DOCTOR DOLITTLE'S
POST OFFICE

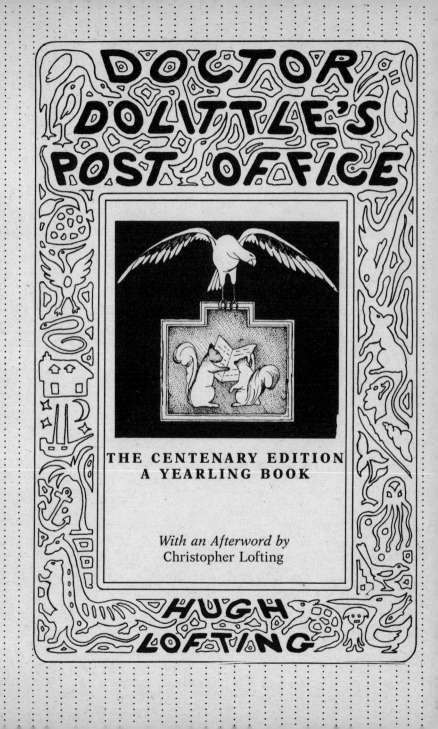

DOCTOR DOLITTLE'S POST OFFICE

THE CENTENARY EDITION
A YEARLING BOOK

With an Afterword by
Christopher Lofting

HUGH LOFTING

Published by
Dell Publishing
a division of
The Bantam Doubleday Dell Publishing Group, Inc.
666 Fifth Avenue
New York, New York 10103

ISBN: 0-440-40096-1

Printed in the United States of America

October 1988

10 9 8 7 6 5 4 3 2 1

CW

· Contents ·

· Illustrations ·

DOCTOR DOLITTLE'S POST OFFICE

PROLOGUE

Nearly all of the history of Doctor Dolittle's post office took place when he was returning from a voyage to West Africa. Therefore I will begin from the place where the Doctor turned his ship toward home again and set sail for Puddleby-on-the-Marsh.

Some time before this the pushmi-pullyu, the remarkable two-headed animal, after a long stay in England, had grown a little homesick for Africa. And although he was tremendously fond of the Doctor and never wanted to leave him altogether, he asked him one winter day when the weather was particularly cold and disagreeable if he would mind running down to Africa for a holiday—just for a week or two.

The Doctor readily agreed because he hadn't been on a voyage in a long while and he felt he too needed a change from the chilly December days of England.

So he started off. Besides the pushmi-pullyu he took Dab-Dab the duck, Jip the dog, Gub-Gub the pig, Too-Too the owl, and the white mouse—the same good company he had had with him on his adventurous return from the Land of the Monkeys. For this trip the Doctor bought a little sailing boat—very old and battered and worn, but a good sound craft for bad weather.

They sailed away down to the south coast of the Bight of Benin. There they visited many African kingdoms and strange places. And while they were ashore the pushmi-pullyu had a chance to wander freely through his old grazing grounds. And he enjoyed his holiday thoroughly.

One morning the Doctor was delighted to see his old friends the swallows gathering once more about his ship at anchor for their yearly flight to England. They asked him whether he too was returning; because if so, they said, they would accompany him, the same as they had done when he was escaping from the Kingdom of Jolliginki.

As the pushmi-pullyu was now quite ready to leave, the Doctor thanked the swallows and told them he would be delighted to have their company. Then for the remainder of that day all was hustle and hurry and bustle, getting the ship provisioned and making preparations for the long trip back to England.

By the following morning everything was in readiness to put to sea. The anchor was drawn up and with all sail set the Doctor's ship moved northward before a favorable wind. And it is from this point that my story begins.

PART ONE

· Chapter 1 ·
ZUZANA

One morning in the first week of the return voyage when John Dolittle and his animals were all sitting at breakfast around the big table in the cabin, one of the swallows came down and said that he wanted to speak to the Doctor.

John Dolittle at once left the table and went out into the passage where he found the swallow leader himself, a very neat, trim little bird with long, long wings and sharp, snappy black eyes. Speedy-the-Skimmer he was called—a name truly famous throughout the whole of the feathered world. He was the champion flycatcher and aerial acrobat of Europe, Africa, Asia, and America. For years every summer he had won all the flying races, having broken his own record only last year by crossing the Atlantic in eleven and a half hours—at a speed of over two hundred miles an hour.

"Well, Speedy," said John Dolittle. "What is it?"

"Doctor," said the little bird in a mysterious whisper, "we have sighted a canoe about a mile ahead of the ship

3

and a little to the eastward, with a woman alone in it. She is weeping bitterly and isn't paddling the canoe at all. She is several miles from land—ten, at least, I should say— because at the moment we are crossing the Bay of Fantippo and can only just see the shore of Africa. She is really in dangerous straits, with such a little bit of a boat that far out at sea. But she doesn't seem to care. She's just sitting in the bottom of the canoe, crying as if she didn't mind what happens to her. I wish you would come and speak to her, for we fear she is in great trouble."

"All right," said the Doctor. "Fly slowly on to where the canoe is and I will steer the ship to follow you."

So John Dolittle went up on deck and by steering the boat after the guiding swallows he presently saw a small, dark canoe rising and falling on the waves. It looked so tiny on the wide face of the waters that it could be taken for a log or a stick—or, indeed, missed altogether, unless you were close enough to see it. In the canoe sat a woman with her head bowed down upon her knees.

"What's the matter?" shouted the Doctor, as soon as he was near enough to make the woman hear. "Why have you come so far from the land? Don't you know that you are in great danger if a storm should come up?"

Slowly the woman raised her head.

"Go away," said she, "and leave me to my sorrow. Haven't you all done me enough harm?"

John Dolittle steered the boat up closer still and continued to talk to the woman in a kindly way. But she seemed for a long time to mistrust him. Little by little, however, the Doctor won her confidence and at last, still weeping bitterly, she told him her story.

These were the days, you must understand, when slavery

was being done away with. To capture, to buy, or to sell slaves had, in fact, been strictly forbidden by most governments. But certain bad men still came down to the west coast of Africa and captured or bought slaves secretly and took them away in ships to other lands to work on cotton and tobacco plantations. Some African kings sold prisoners they had taken in war to these men and made a great deal of money that way.

Well, this woman in the canoe belonged to a tribe that had been at war with the King of Fantippo—an African kingdom situated on the coast near which the swallows had seen the canoe.

And in this war the King of Fantippo had taken many prisoners, among whom was the woman's husband. Shortly after the war was over some men in a ship had called at the Kingdom of Fantippo to see if they could buy slaves for tobacco plantations. And when the King heard how much money they were willing to give for slaves he thought he would sell them the prisoners he had taken in the war.

This woman's name was Zuzana and her husband was a very strong and fine-looking man. The King of Fantippo would have kept Zuzana's husband for this reason, because he liked to have strong men at his court. But the slave traders also wanted strong men, for they could do a lot of work on the plantations. And they offered the King of Fantippo an especially high price for Zuzana's husband. And the King had sold him.

Zuzana described to the Doctor how she had followed the man's ship a long way out in a canoe, imploring them to give her back her husband. But they had only laughed at her and gone on their way. And their ship had soon passed out of sight.

That was why, she said, she hated all foreign men and had not wanted to speak to the Doctor when he had hailed her canoe.

The Doctor was dreadfully angry when he had heard the story. And he asked Zuzana how long ago was it that the slaver's ship bearing her husband had left.

She told him it was half an hour ago. Without her husband, she said, life meant nothing to her, and when the ship had passed from view, going northward along the coast, she had burst into tears and just let the canoe drift, not even having the heart to paddle back to land.

The Doctor told the woman that no matter what it cost he was going to help her. And he was all for speeding up his ship and going in chase of the slave boat right away. But Dab-Dab the duck warned him that his boat was very slow and that its sails could be easily seen by the slavers, who would never allow it to come near them.

So the Doctor put down his anchor and, leaving the ship where it was, got into the woman's canoe. Then, calling to the swallows to help him as guides, he set off northward along the coast, looking into all the bays and behind all the islands for the slave ship which had taken Zuzana's husband.

But after many hours of fruitless search night began to come on and the swallows who were acting as guides could no longer see big distances, for there was no moon.

Poor Zuzana began weeping some more when the Doctor said he would have to give up for the night.

"By morning," said she, "the ship of the wicked slave

dealers will be many miles away and I shall never get my husband back. Alas! Alas!"

The Doctor comforted her as best he could, saying that if he failed he would get her another husband, just as good. But she didn't seem to care for that idea and went on wailing, "Alas! Alas!"

She made such a noise that the Doctor couldn't get to sleep on the bottom of the canoe—which wasn't very comfortable, anyway. So he had to sit up and listen. Some of the swallows were still with him, sitting on the edge of the canoe. And the famous Skimmer, the leader, was also there. They and the Doctor were talking over what they could do, when suddenly the Skimmer said, "Sh! Look!" and pointed out to the westward over the dark, heaving sea.

Even Zuzana stopped her wailing and turned to look. And there, away out on the dim, black edge of the ocean, they could see a tiny light.

"A ship!" cried the Doctor.

"Yes," said Speedy, "that's a ship, sure enough. I wonder if it's another slave ship."

"Well, if it's a slave ship, it's not the one we're looking for," said the Doctor, "because it's in the wrong direction. The one we're after went northward."

"Listen, Doctor," said Speedy-the-Skimmer, "suppose I fly over to it and see what kind of a ship it is and come back and tell you. Who knows? It might be able to help us."

"All right, Speedy. Thank you," said the Doctor.

So the Skimmer sped off into the darkness toward the tiny light far out to sea, while the Doctor fell to wondering how his own ship was getting on, which he had left at anchor some miles down the coast to the southward.

After twenty minutes had gone by John Dolittle began to get worried because the Skimmer, with his tremendous speed, should have had time to get there and back long ago.

But soon, with a flirt of the wings, the famous leader made a neat circle in the darkness overhead and dropped, light as a feather, on to the Doctor's knee.

"Well," said John Dolittle, "what kind of a ship was it?"

"It's a big ship," panted the Skimmer, "with tall, high masts and, I should judge, a fast one. But it is coming this way and it is sailing with great care, afraid, I imagine, of shallows and sandbars. It is a very neat ship, smart and new-looking all over. And there are great big guns—cannons—looking out of little doors in her sides. The men on her, too, are all well dressed in smart blue clothes—not like ordinary seamen at all. And on the ship's hull was painted some lettering—her name, I suppose. Of course, I couldn't read it. But I remember what it looked like. Give me your hand and I'll show you."

Then the Skimmer, with one of his claws, began tracing out some letters on the Doctor's palm. Before he had got very far John Dolittle sprang up, nearly overturning the canoe.

"HMS!" he cried. "That means Her Majesty's Ship. It's a man-o'-war—a navy vessel. The very thing we want to deal with slave traders!"

· Chapter 2 ·

THE DOCTOR'S RECEPTION
ON THE WARSHIP

Then the Doctor and Zuzana started to paddle their canoe for all they were worth in the direction of the light. The night was calm, but the long swell of the ocean swung the little canoe up and down like a seesaw and it needed all Zuzana's skill to keep it in a straight line.

After about an hour had gone by the Doctor noticed that the ship they were trying to reach was no longer coming toward them, but seemed to have stopped. And when he finally came up beneath its towering shape in the darkness he saw the reason why—the man-o'-war had run into his own ship, which he had left at anchor with no lights. However, the navy vessel had fortunately been going so carefully that no serious damage, it seemed, had been done to either ship.

Finding a rope ladder hanging on the side of the man-o'-war, John Dolittle climbed up it, with Zuzana, and went aboard to see the captain.

He found the captain strutting about on the quarterdeck, mumbling to himself.

"Good evening," said the Doctor politely. "Nice weather we're having."

The captain came up to him and shook his fist in his face.

"Are you the owner of that Noah's Ark down there?" he stormed, pointing to the other ship alongside.

"Er—yes—temporarily," said the Doctor. "Why?"

"Well, will you be so good," snarled the captain, his face all out of shape with rage, "as to tell me what in thunder you mean by leaving your old junk at anchor on a dark night without any lights? What kind of a sailor are you? Here I bring Her Majesty's latest cruiser after Jimmie Bones, the slave trader—been hunting him for weeks, I have—and, as though the beastly coast wasn't difficult enough as it is, I bump into a craft riding at anchor with no lights. Luckily, I was going slow, taking soundings, or we might have gone down with all hands. I hallooed to your ship and got no answer. So I go aboard her, with pistols ready, thinking maybe she's a slaver, trying to play tricks on me. I creep all over the ship, but not a soul do I meet. At last in the cabin I find a pig—*asleep in an arm-chair!* Do you usually leave your craft in the charge of a pig, with orders to go to sleep? If you own the ship, why aren't you on her? Where have you been?"

"I was out canoeing with a lady," said the Doctor, and he smiled comfortingly at Zuzana, who was beginning to weep again.

"Canoeing with a lady!" spluttered the captain. "Well, I'll be—"

"Yes," said the Doctor. "Let me introduce you. This is Zuzana, Captain—er—"

HUGH LOFTING

" 'Where have you been?' "

But the captain interrupted him by calling for a sailor,
who stood near.

"I'll teach you to leave Noah's Ark at anchor on the
high seas for the navy to bump into, my fine deep-sea
philanderer! Think the shipping laws are made for a
joke? Here," he turned to the sailor, who had come in
answer to his call, "Master-at-arms, put this man under
arrest."

"Aye, aye, sir," said the master-at-arms. And before the

Doctor knew it he had handcuffs fastened firmly on his wrists.

"But this lady was in distress," said the Doctor. "I was in such a hurry I forgot all about lighting the ship. In fact, it wasn't dark yet when I left."

"Take him below!" roared the captain. "Take him below before I kill him."

And the poor Doctor was dragged away by the master-at-arms toward a stair leading to the lower decks. But at the head of the stairs he caught hold of the handrail and hung on long enough to shout back to the captain:

"I could tell you where Jimmie Bones is, if I wanted to."

"What's that?" snorted the captain. "Here, bring him back! What was that you said?"

"I said," murmured the Doctor, getting his handkerchief out and blowing his nose with his handcuffed hands, "that I could tell you where Jimmie Bones is—if I wanted to."

"Jimmie Bones, the slaver?" cried the captain. "That's the man the government has sent me after. Where is he?"

"My memory doesn't work very well while my hands are tied," said the Doctor quietly, nodding toward the handcuffs. "Possibly if you took these things off I might remember."

"Oh, excuse me," said the captain, his manner changing at once. "Master-at-arms, release the prisoner."

"Aye, aye, sir," said the sailor, removing the handcuffs from the Doctor's wrists and turning to go.

"Oh, and by the way," the captain called after him, "bring a chair up on deck. Perhaps our visitor is tired."

Then John Dolittle told the captain the whole story of Zuzana and her troubles. And all the other officers on the ship gathered around to listen.

"And I have no doubt," the Doctor ended, "that this slaver who took away the woman's husband was no other than Jimmie Bones, the man you are after."

"Quite so," said the captain. "I know he is somewhere around the coast. But where is he now? He's a difficult fish to catch."

"He has gone northward," said the Doctor. "But your ship is fast and should be able to overtake him. If he hides in some of these bays and creeks I have several birds here with me who can, as soon as it is light, seek him out for us and tell us where he is."

The captain looked with astonishment into the faces of his listening officers, who all smiled unbelievingly.

"What do you mean—birds?" the captain asked. "Pigeons, trained canaries, or something?"

"No," said the Doctor, "I mean the swallows who are going back to England for the summer. They very kindly offered to guide my ship home. They're friends of mine, you see."

This time the officers all burst out laughing and tapped their foreheads knowingly to show they thought the Doctor was crazy. And the captain, thinking he was being made a fool of, flew into a rage once more and was all for having the Doctor arrested again.

But the officer who was second in command whispered in the captain's ear, "Why not take the old fellow along and let him try, sir? Our course was northward, anyway. I seem to remember hearing something, when I was attached to the Home Fleet, about an old chap in the west counties who had some strange powers with beasts and birds. I have no doubt this is he. Dolittle, he was called. He seems harmless enough. There's just a chance he may be of some assistance to us. The natives evidently trust him or the woman wouldn't have come with him—you know how scared they are of putting to sea with strange men."

After a moment's thought the captain turned to the Doctor again.

"You sound clean crazy to me, my good man. But if you can put me in the way of capturing Jimmie Bones, the slaver, I don't care what means you use to do it. As soon as the day breaks we will get under way. But if you are just amusing yourself at the expense of Her Majesty's Navy, I warn you it will be the worst day's work for yourself you ever did. Now go and put riding lights on that Ark of yours and tell the pig that if he lets them go out he shall be made into rashers of bacon for the officers' mess."

There was much laughter and joking as the Doctor climbed over the side and went back to his own ship to get his lights lit. But the next morning when he came back to the man-o'-war—and about a thousand swallows came with him—the officers of Her Majesty's Navy were not nearly so inclined to make fun of him.

The sun was just rising over the distant coast of Africa and it was as beautiful a morning as you could wish to see.

Speedy-the-Skimmer had arranged plans with the Doctor overnight. And long before the great warship pulled up her anchor and swung around upon her course the famous swallow leader was miles ahead with a band of picked hunters, exploring up creeks and examining all the hollows of the coast where the slave trader might be hiding.

Speedy had agreed with the Doctor upon a sort of overhead telegraph system to be carried on by the swallows. And as soon as the millions of little birds had spread themselves out in a line along the coast, so that the sky was

"The birds spread themselves out along the coast"

speckled with them as far as the eye could reach, they began passing messages by whistling to one another, all the way from the scouts in front, back to the Doctor on the warship, to give news of how the hunt was progressing.

And somewhere about noon word came through that Bones's slave ship had been sighted behind a long, high cape. Great care must be taken, the message said, because the slave ship was in all readiness to sail at a moment's notice. The slavers had only stopped to get water and look-outs were posted to warn them to return at once, if necessary.

When the Doctor told this to the captain the man-o'-war changed her course still closer inshore, to keep behind the cover of the long cape. All the sailors were warned to keep very quiet, so the navy ship could sneak up on the slaver unaware.

Now, the captain, expecting the slavers to put up a fight, also gave orders to get the guns ready. And just as they were about to round the long cape one of the silly gunners let a gun off by accident.

"Boom!" The shot went rolling and echoing over the silent sea like angry thunder.

Instantly back came word over the swallows' telegraph line that the slavers were warned and were escaping. And, sure enough, when the warship rounded the cape at last, there was the slave ship putting out to sea, with all sail set and a good ten-mile start on the man-o'-war.

· Chapter 3 ·
A GREAT GUNNER

And then began a most exciting sea race. It was now two o'clock in the afternoon and there were not many hours of daylight left.

The captain (after he had finished swearing at the stupid gunner who had let off the gun by accident) realized that if he did not catch up to the slaver before dark came on he would probably lose him altogether. For this Jim Bones was a very sly and clever rascal and he knew the west coast of Africa very well. After dark by running without lights he would easily find some nook or corner to hide in—or double back on his course and be miles away before morning came.

So the captain gave orders that all possible speed was to be made. These were the days when steam was first used on ships, together with the sails, to help the power of the wind. Of this vessel, HMS *Violet*, the captain was very proud. And he was most anxious that the *Violet* should have the honor of catching Bones, the slaver, who for so long had been defying the navy by carrying on slave trade after it had been forbidden. So the *Violet's* steam engines were put to work their hardest. Thick, black smoke rolled out of her funnels and darkened the blue sea and smudged up her lovely white sails humming tight in the breeze.

Then the engine boy, also anxious that his ship should have the honor of capturing Bones, tied down the safety valve on the steam engine, to make her go faster, and then went up on deck to see the show. And soon, of course, one of the *Violet's* brand-new boilers burst with a terrific bang and made an awful mess of the engine room.

But, being a full-rigged man-o'-war, the *Violet* was still a pretty speedy sailer. And on she went, furiously plowing the waves and slowly gaining on the slave ship.

However, the crafty Bones, with so big a start, was not easy to overtake. And soon the sun began to set and the captain frowned and stamped his feet. For with darkness he knew his enemy would be safe.

Down below among the crew, the man who had fired the gun by accident was having a terrible time. All his companions were setting on him and mobbing him for being such a duffer as to warn Bones—who would now almost certainly escape. The distance from the slaver was still too great to use the kind of guns they had in those days. But when the captain saw darkness creeping over the sea and his enemy escaping, he gave orders to man the guns, anyway—although he hadn't the least hope that his shots would hit the slaver at that distance.

Now, Speedy-the-Skimmer, as soon as the race had begun, had come on to the warship to take a rest. And he happened to be talking to the Doctor when the order to man the guns came down from the captain. So the Doctor and Speedy went below to watch the guns being fired.

They found an air of quiet but great excitement there. Each gunner was leaning on his gun, aiming it, watching the enemy's ship in the distance and waiting for the order to fire. The poor man who had been mobbed by his fellows was still almost in tears at his own stupid mistake.

Suddenly an officer shouted *"Fire!"* And with a crash that shook the ship from stem to stern eight big cannonballs went whistling out across the water.

But not one hit the slave ship. *Splash! Splash! Splash!* They fell harmlessly into the water.

"The light's too bad," grumbled the gunners. "Who could hit anything two miles away in this rotten light?"

Then Speedy whispered in the Doctor's ear, "Ask them to let me fire a gun. My sight is better than theirs for bad light."

But just at that moment the order came from the captain, *"Cease firing!"* And the men left their places.

As soon as their backs were turned Speedy jumped on top of one of the guns and, straddling his short, white legs apart, he cast his beady little black eyes along the aiming sights. Then with his wings he signaled to the Doctor behind him to swing the gun this way and that, so as to aim it the way he wanted.

"Fire!" said Speedy. And the Doctor fired.

"What in thunder's this?" roared the captain from the quarterdeck as the shot rang out. "Didn't I give the order to cease firing?"

But the second in command plucked him by the sleeve and pointed across the water. Speedy's cannonball had cut the slaver's mainmast clean in two and brought the sails down in a heap upon the deck!

" *'Fire!'* said Speedy"

"Holy smoke!" cried the captain. "We've hit him! Look, Bones is flying the signal of surrender!"

Then the captain, who a moment before was all for punishing the man who had fired without orders, wanted to know who it was that aimed that marvelous shot which brought the slaver to a standstill. And the Doctor was going to tell him it was Speedy.

But the Skimmer whispered in his ear, "Don't bother, Doctor. He would never believe you, anyway. It was the gun of the man that made the mistake before that we used. Let him take the credit. They'll likely give him a medal, and then he'll feel better."

And now all was excitement aboard the *Violet* as they approached the slave boat lying crippled in the sea. Bones, the captain, with his crew of eleven other ruffians, was taken prisoner and put down in the cells of the warship. Then the Doctor, with Zuzana, some sailors, and an officer, went on to the slave ship. Entering the hold, they found the place packed with slaves with chains on them. And Zuzana immediately recognized her husband and wept all over him with joy.

The men were at once freed from their chains and brought on to the man-o'-war. Then the slave ship was taken in tow by the *Violet*. And that was the end of Mr. Bones's slave trading.

Then there was much rejoicing and hand shaking and congratulation on board the warship. And a grand dinner was prepared for the slaves on the main deck. But John Dolittle, Zuzana, and her husband were invited to the of- ficers' mess, where their health was drunk in port wine and speeches were made by the captain and the Doctor.

The next day, as soon as it was light, the warship went cruising down the coast again, putting people ashore in their own particular countries.

This took considerable time, because Bones, it seemed, had collected slaves from a great many different places. And it was after noon before the Doctor, Zuzana, and her husband were returned to John Dolittle's ship, which still had her lights faithfully burning in the middle of the day.

Then the captain shook hands with the Doctor and thanked him for the great assistance he had given Her

Majesty's Navy. And he asked him for his address in England because he said he was going to tell the government about him and the Queen would most likely want to make him a knight or give him a medal or something. But the Doctor said he would rather have a pound of tea instead. He hadn't tasted tea in several months and the kind they had in the officers' mess was very good.

So the captain gave him five pounds of the best China tea and thanked him again in the name of the Queen and the government.

Then the *Violet* swung her great bow around to the north once more and sailed away for England, while the blue-jackets crowded the rail and sent three hearty cheers for the Doctor ringing across the sea.

And now Jip, Dab-Dab, Gub-Gub, Too-Too, and the rest of them gathered around John Dolittle and wanted to hear all about his adventures. And it was teatime before he had done telling them. So the Doctor asked Zuzana and her husband to take tea with him before they went ashore.

This they were glad to do. And the Doctor made the tea himself and it was very excellent. Over the tea Zuzana and her husband (whose name was Begwe) were conversing about the Kingdom of Fantippo.

"I don't think we ought to go back there," said Begwe. "I don't mind being a soldier in the Fantippo army, but suppose some other slaver comes along. Maybe the king would sell me again. Did you send that letter to our cousin?"

"Yes," said Zuzana. "But I don't think he ever got it. Because no answer came."

The Doctor asked Zuzana how she had sent the letter. And then she explained to him that when Bones had

"The bluejackets crowded to the rail"

offered a big price for Begwe and the king had been tempted to sell him, she had told the king she would get twelve oxen and thirty goats from a rich cousin in their own country if he would only wait till she had written to him. Now, the King of Fantippo was very fond of oxen and goats—cattle being considered as good as money in his land. And he promised Zuzana that if she got the twelve oxen and thirty goats in two days' time her husband should be a free man, instead of being sold to the slavers.

So Zuzana had hurried to a professional letter writer (the common people of those tribes couldn't write for themselves, you see) and had a letter written, begging their cousin to send the goats and oxen to the king without delay. Then she had taken the letter to the Fantippo post office and sent it off.

But the two days went by and no answer came—and no cattle. Then poor Begwe had been sold to Bones's men.

· Chapter 4 ·

THE ROYAL MAILS OF FANTIPPO

Now, this Fantippo post office of which Zuzana had spoken to the Doctor was rather peculiar. For one thing, it was, of course, quite unusual to find a post office or regular mails of any kind in a tiny African kingdom. And the way such a thing had come about was this:

A few years before this voyage of the Doctor's there had been a great deal of talk in most parts of the world about mails and how much it should cost for a letter to go from one country to another. And in England it had been agreed that a penny a letter should be the regular rate charged for mails from one part of the British Isles to another. Of course, for especially heavy letters you had to pay more. Then stamps were made—penny stamps, twopenny stamps, twopence-halfpenny stamps, sixpenny stamps, and shilling stamps. And each was a different color and they were beautifully engraved and most of them had a picture of the Queen on them—some with her crown on her head and some without.

And France and the United States and all the other countries started doing the same thing.

Now, it happened one day that a ship called at the coast of West Africa, and delivered a letter for Koko, the King of Fantippo. King Koko had never seen a stamp before, and sending for a merchant who lived in his town, he asked him what queen's face was this on the stamp that the letter bore.

Then the merchant explained to him the whole idea of penny postage and government mails. And he told him that in England all you had to do when you wanted to send a letter to any part of the world was to put a stamp on the envelope with the queen's head on it and place it in a letter box on the street corner, and it would be carried to the place to which you addressed it.

"Aha!" said the King. "A new kind of magic. I understand. Very good. The High Kingdom of Fantippo shall have a post office of its own. And *my* serene and beautiful face shall be on all the stamps and *my* letters shall travel by faster magic than any of them."

Then King Koko of Fantippo, being a very vain man, had a fine lot of stamps made with his pictures on them, some with his crown on and some without; some smiling, some frowning; some with himself on horseback, some with himself on a bicycle. But the stamp which he was most proud of was the tenpenny stamp which bore a picture of himself playing golf—a game which he had just recently learned from some Scotsmen who were mining for gold in his kingdom.

And he had letter boxes made, just the way the trader had told him they had in England, and he set them up at the corners of the streets and told his people that all they had to do was to put one of his stamps on their letters, poke them into these boxes, and they would travel to any corner of the earth they wished.

But presently the people began complaining that they had been robbed. They had paid good money for the stamps, they said, trusting in their magic power, and they had put their letters in the boxes at the corners of the streets as they had been told. But one day a cow had rubbed her neck against one of the letter boxes and burst it open, and inside there were all the people's letters, which had not traveled one inch from where they put them!

Then the King was very angry and, calling for the trader, he said, "You have been fooling My Majesty. These stamps you speak of have no magic power at all. Explain!"

Then the trader told him that it was not through magic in the stamps or boxes that letters traveled by mail. But proper post offices had mailmen, or postmen, who collected the letters out of these boxes. And he went on to explain to the King all the other duties of a post office and the things that made letters go.

So then the King, who was a persevering man, said that Fantippo should have its post office, anyway. And he sent to England for hundreds of postmen's uniforms and caps. And when these arrived he dressed a lot of the men up in them and set them to work as postmen.

But the men found the heavy uniforms dreadfully hot for Fantippo weather, where they wear only a string of beads. And they left off the uniforms and wore only the caps. That is how the Fantippo postman's uniform came to be a smart cap, a string of beads, and a mailbag.

Then when King Koko had got his mailmen, the Royal Fantippo post office began really working. Letters were collected from the boxes at street corners and sent off when ships called; and incoming mail was delivered at the doors of the houses in Fantippo three times a day. The post office became the busiest place in town.

Now, the peoples of West Africa have different tastes in dress. They love bright things. And some Fantippo dandy started the idea of using up old stamps off letters by making suits of clothes out of them. They looked very showy and smart and a suit of this kind made of stamps became a valuable possession among the natives.

About this time, too, in other parts of the world the craze or hobby of collecting stamps arose. In England and America and other countries people began buying stamp albums and pasting stamps in them. A rare stamp became quite valuable.

And it happened that one day two men whose hobby was collecting stamps came to Fantippo in a ship. The one stamp they were both most anxious to get for their collections was the "twopenny Fantippo red," a stamp which the King had given up printing—for the reason that the picture of himself on it wasn't handsome enough. And because he had given up printing it, it became very rare.

As soon as these two men stepped ashore at Fantippo, a porter came up to them to carry their bags. And right in the middle of the porter's chest the collectors spied the twopenny Fantippo red! Then both of the stamp collectors offered to buy the stamp. And as each was anxious to have it for his collection, before long they were offering high prices for it, bidding against one another.

King Koko got to hear of this and he called up one of these stamp collectors and asked him why men should offer high prices for one old used stamp. And the man explained to him this new craze for stamp collecting that was sweeping over the world.

So King Koko decided it would be a good idea if *he* sold stamps for collections—much better business than selling them at his post office for letters. And after that whenever a ship came into the harbor of Fantippo he sent his postmaster general—a very grand man, who wore *two* strings of beads, a postman's cap, and no mailbag—out to the ship with stamps to sell for collections.

Such a roaring trade was done in this way that the King set the stamp-printing presses to work more busily than ever, so that a whole new set of Fantippo stamps should be ready for sale by the time the same ship called again on her way home to England.

But with this new trade in selling stamps for stamp collections, and not for proper mailing purposes, the Fantippo mail service was neglected and became very bad.

Now Doctor Dolittle, while Zuzana was talking over the tea about her letter that she had sent to her cousin—and to which no answer had ever come—suddenly remembered something. On one of his earlier voyages the passenger ship by which he had been traveling had stopped outside this same harbor of Fantippo, although no passengers had gone ashore. And a postman had come aboard to sell a most elegant lot of new green and violet stamps. The Doctor, being at the time a great stamp collector, had bought three whole sets.

And he realized now, as he listened to Zuzana, what was wrong with the Fantippo post office and why she had never gotten an answer to the letter that would have saved her husband from slavery.

As Zuzana and Begwe rose to go, for it was beginning to

get dark, the Doctor noticed a canoe setting out toward his ship from the shore. And in it, when it got near, he saw King Koko himself, coming to the boat with stamps to sell.

So the Doctor got talking to the King and he told him in plain language that he ought to be ashamed of his post office. Then, giving him a cup of China tea, he explained to him how Zuzana's letter had probably never been delivered to her cousin.

The King listened attentively and understood how his post office had been at fault. And he invited the Doctor to come ashore with Zuzana and Begwe and arrange the post office for him and put it in order so it would work properly.

· Chapter 5 ·

THE VOYAGE DELAYED

After some persuasion the Doctor consented to this proposal feeling that perhaps he could do some good.

He found the town of Fantippo very different from any of the African villages or settlements he had ever visited. It was quite large, almost a city. It was bright and cheerful to look at and the people, like their King, all seemed very kind and jolly.

The Doctor was introduced to all the chief men of the Fantippo nation and later he was taken to see the post office.

This he found in a terrible state. There were letters everywhere—on the floors, in old drawers, knocking about on desks, even lying on the pavement outside the post-office door. The Doctor explained to the King that in properly run post offices the letters that had stamps on were treated with respect and care. It was no wonder, he said, that Zuzana's letter had never been delivered to her cousin, if this was the way they took care of the mails.

Then King Koko again begged him to take charge of the post office and try to get it running in proper order. And the Doctor said he would see what he could do.

But after many hours of terrific labor, John Dolittle saw that setting the Fantippo post office to rights would take weeks at least. He told this to the King, so the Doctor's ship was brought into the harbor and put safely at anchor and the animals were all taken ashore. A nice new house on the main street was given over to the Doctor for himself and his pets to live in while the work of straightening out the Fantippo mails was going on.

After ten days John Dolittle got what is called the *domestic mails* in pretty good shape. Domestic mails are those that carry letters from one part of a country to another part of the same country, or from one part of a city to another. The mails that carry letters outside the country to foreign lands are called *foreign mails*. To have a regular and good service of foreign mails in the Fantippo post office the Doctor found a hard problem because the mail ships that could carry letters abroad did not come very often to this port. Fantippo, although King Koko was most proud of it, was not considered a very important country among the larger nations, and two or three ships a year were all that ever called there.

Now, one day, very early in the morning, when the Doctor was lying in bed, wondering what he could do about the foreign mail service, Dab-Dab and Jip brought him in his breakfast on a tray and told him there was a swallow outside who wanted to give him a message from Speedy-the-Skimmer. John Dolittle had the swallow brought in and the little bird sat on the foot of his bed while he ate his breakfast.

" 'Good morning! What can I do for you?' "

"Good morning," said the Doctor, cracking open the top of a hard-boiled egg. "What can I do for you?"

"Speedy would like to know," said the swallow, "how long you expect to stay in this country. He doesn't want to complain, you understand—nor do any of us—but this journey of yours is taking longer than we thought it would. You see, there was the delay while we hunted out Bones the slaver, and now it seems likely you will be busy with this post office for some weeks yet. Ordinarily we would have been in England long before this, getting the nests ready for the new season's families. We cannot put off the nesting season, you know. Of course, you understand we are not complaining, don't you? But this delay is making things rather awkward for us."

"Oh, quite, quite. I understand perfectly," said the Doctor, poking salt into his egg with a bone egg spoon. "I am dreadfully sorry. But why didn't Speedy bring the message himself?"

"I suppose he didn't like to," said the swallow. "Thought you'd be offended, perhaps."

"Oh, not in the least," said the Doctor. "You birds have been most helpful to me. Tell Speedy I'll come to see him as soon as I've got my trousers on and we'll talk it over. Something can be arranged, I have no doubt."

"Very good, Doctor," said the swallow, turning to go. "I'll tell the Skimmer what you say."

"By the way," said John Dolittle, "I've been trying to think where I've seen your face before. Did you ever build your nest in my stable in Puddleby?"

"No," said the bird. "But I am the swallow that brought you the message from the monkeys that time they were sick."

"Oh, to be sure—of course," cried the Doctor. "I knew I had seen you somewhere. I never forget faces. You had a pretty hard time coming to England in the winter, didn't you—snow on the ground and all that sort of thing. Very plucky of you to undertake it."

"Yes, it was a hard trip," said the swallow. "I came near freezing to death more than once. But something had to be done. The monkeys would most likely have been wiped right out if we hadn't gotten you."

"How was it that you were the one chosen to bring the message?" asked the Doctor.

"Well," said the swallow, "Speedy did want to do it himself. He's frightfully brave, you know—and fast as lightning. But the other swallows wouldn't let him. They said he was too valuable. Because, besides being brave and fast, he's the cleverest leader we ever had. Whenever the swallows are in trouble he always thinks of a way out. He's a born leader. He flies quick and he thinks quick."

"Humph!" murmured the Doctor, as he thoughtfully brushed the toast crumbs off the bedclothes. "But why did they pick you to bring the message?"

"They didn't," said the swallow. "We nearly all of us volunteered for the job, but the Skimmer said the only fair way was to draw lots. So we got a number of small leaves and we took the stalks off all of them except one. And we put the leaves in an old coconut shell and shook them up. Then with our eyes shut, we began picking them out. The swallow who picked the leaf with the stalk on it was to carry the message to England—and I picked the leaf with the stalk on. Before I started off on the trip I kissed my wife good-bye because I really never expected to get back alive. Still, I'm kind of glad the lot fell to me."

"Why?" asked the Doctor, pushing the breakfast tray off his knees and punching the pillows into shape.

"Well, you see," said the swallow, lifting his right leg and showing a tiny red ribbon made of corn silk tied about his ankle, "I got this for it."

"What's that?" asked the Doctor.

"That's to show I've done something brave—and special," said the swallow modestly.

"Oh, I see," said the Doctor. "Like a medal, eh?"

HUGH LOFTING

"They found the Doctor shaving"

"Yes. My name is Quip. It used to be just plain Quip. Now I'm called *Quip-the-Carrier*," said the small bird proudly, gazing down at his little, stubby white leg.

"Splendid, Quip," said the Doctor. "I congratulate you. Now I must be getting up. I've a frightful lot of work to do. Don't forget to tell Speedy I'll meet him on the ship at ten. Good-bye! Oh, and would you mind asking Dab-Dab, as you go out, to clear away the breakfast things? I'm glad you came. You've given me an idea. Good-bye!"

And when Dab-Dab and Jip came to take away the tray they found the Doctor shaving. He was peering into a looking glass, holding the end of his nose and muttering to himself, *"That's* the idea for the Fantippo foreign mail service—I wonder why I never thought of it before. I'll have the fastest overseas mail the world ever saw. Why, of course! That's the idea—*the Swallow Mail!"*

· Chapter 6 ·
NO-MAN'S-LAND

As soon as he was dressed and shaved, the Doctor went down to his ship and met the Skimmer.

"I am terribly sorry, Speedy," said he, "to hear what a lot of trouble I have been giving you birds by my delay here. But I really feel that the business of the post office ought to be attended to. It's in a shocking state."

"I know," said Speedy. "And if we could we would have nested right here in this country and not bothered about going to England this year. But, you see, we swallows can't nest very well in trees. We like houses and barns and buildings to nest in."

"Couldn't you use the houses of Fantippo?" asked the Doctor.

"Not very well," said Speedy. "They're so small and noisy —with the native children playing around them all day. The eggs and young ones wouldn't be safe for a minute. And, then, they're not built right for us—mostly made of grass, the roofs sloping wrong, the eaves too near the ground, and all that. What we like are solid English buildings, quiet buildings like old barns and stables. We like people, you understand—in their right place. But nesting mother birds must have quiet."

"Humph! I see," said the Doctor. "Of course, myself, I rather enjoy the jolliness of these Fantippos. But I can quite see your point. By the way, how would my old ship do? This ought to be quiet enough for you here. There's nobody living on it now. And, look, it has heaps of cracks and holes and corners in it where you could build your nests. What do you think?"

"That would be splendid," said Speedy, "if you think you won't be needing the boat for some weeks. Of course, it would never do if, after we had the nests built and the eggs laid, you were to pull up the anchor and sail away—the young ones would get seasick."

"No, of course not," said the Doctor. "But there will be no fear of my leaving for some time yet. You could have the whole ship to yourselves and nobody will disturb you."

"All right," said Speedy. "Then I'll tell the swallows to get on with the nest building right away. But, of course, we'll go on to England with you when you are ready, to show you the way—and also to teach the young birds how to get there, too. You see, each year's new birds make their first trip back from England to Africa with us grown ones. They have to make the first journey under our guidance."

"Very good," said the Doctor. "Then that settles that. Now I must get back to the post office. The ship is yours. But as soon as the nesting is over, come and let me know because I have a very special idea I want to tell you about."

So the Doctor's boat was now turned into a nesting ship for the swallows. Calmly she stood at anchor in the quiet waters of Fantippo harbor while thousands and thousands

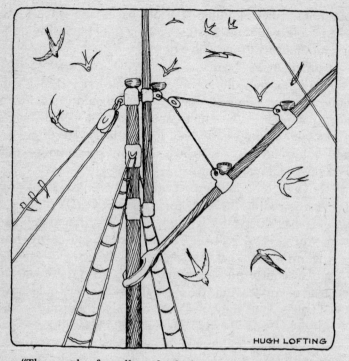

HUGH LOFTING

"Thousands of swallows built their nests in her rigging"

of swallows built their nests in her rigging, in her ventilators, in her portholes, and in every crack and corner of her.

No one went near her and the swallows had her to themselves. And they agreed afterward that they found her the best place for nesting they had ever used.

In a very short time the ship presented a curious and extraordinary sight, with the mud nests stuck all over her and birds flying in thousands around her masts, coming and going, building homes and feeding young ones.

And the farmers in England that year said the coming winter would be a hard one because the swallows had done their nesting abroad before they arrived and only spent a few weeks of the autumn in the north.

Now, it happened one day that the Doctor came to the post office, as usual, at nine o'clock in the morning. (He had to get there at that time because if he didn't the postmen didn't start working.) And outside the post office he found Jip gnawing a bone on the pavement. Something curious about the bone struck the Doctor, who was, of course, being a naturalist, quite a specialist in bones. He asked Jip to let him look at it.

"Why, this is extraordinary!" said the Doctor, examining the bone with great care. "I did not know that this class of animals was still to be found in Africa. Where did you get this bone, Jip?"

"Over in No-Man's-Land," said Jip. "There are lots of bones there."

"And where might No-Man's-Land be?" said John Dolittle.

"No-Man's-Land is that round island just outside the harbor," said Jip. "You know, the one that looks like a plum pudding."

"Oh, yes," said the Doctor. "I know the island you mean. It's only a short distance from the mainland. But I hadn't heard that that was the name of it. Humph! If you'll lend me this bone a while, Jip, I think I'll go to see the King about it."

So, taking the bone, John Dolittle went off to call on King Koko, and Jip asked if he might come along. They found the King sitting at the palace door, sucking a lollipop—for he, like all the Fantippos, was very fond of sweets.

"Good morning, Your Majesty," said the Doctor. "Do you happen to know what kind of animal this bone belongs to?"

The King examined it, then shook his head. He didn't know much about bones.

"Maybe it's a cow's bone," said he.

"Oh, certainly not," said John Dolittle. "No cow ever had a bone like that. That's a jaw—but not a cow's jaw. Listen, Your Majesty, would you mind lending me a canoe and some paddlers? I want to go over to visit No-Man's-Land."

To the Doctor's astonishment the King choked on his lollipop and nearly fell over his chair backward. Then he ran inside the palace and shut the door.

"How extraordinary!" said John Dolittle, entirely bewildered. "What ails the man?"

"Oh, it's some humbug or other," growled Jip. "Let's go down to the harbor, Doctor, and try to hire a canoe to take us."

So they went down to the water's edge and asked several of the canoesmen to take them over to No-Man's-Land. But everyone they asked got dreadfully frightened and refused to talk when the Doctor told them where he wanted to go. They wouldn't even let him borrow their canoes to go there by himself.

At last they found one very old boatman who loved chatting so much that, although he got terribly scared when John Dolittle mentioned No-Man's-Land, he finally told the Doctor the reason for all this extraordinary behavior.

"That island," said he, "—we don't even mention its

name unless we have to—is the land of evil magic. It is called (the old man whispered it so low the Doctor could scarcely hear him) No-Man's-Land because no man lives there. No man ever even goes there."

"But why?" asked the Doctor.

"Dragons live there!" said the old boatman, his eyes wide and staring. "Enormous horned dragons that spit fire and eat men. If you value your life, never go near that dreadful island."

"But how do you know all this," asked the Doctor, "if nobody has ever been there to see if it's true or not?"

"A thousand years ago," said the old man, "when King Kakaboochi ruled over this land, he put his mother-in-law upon that island to live because she talked too much and he couldn't bear her around the palace. It was arranged that food should be taken to her every week. But the first week that the men went there in canoes they could find no trace of her. While they were seeking her about the island, a dragon suddenly roared out from the bushes and attacked them. They only just escaped with their lives and got back to Fantippo and told King Kakaboochi. A famous wizard was consulted and he said it must have been the King's mother-in-law herself who had been changed into a dragon by some magic spell. Since then she has had many children and the island is peopled with dragons—*whose food is men!* For whenever a canoe approaches, the dragons come down to the shores, breathing flame and destruction. But for many hundreds of years now, no man has set foot upon it. That is why it is called—well, you know."

After he had told this story the old man turned away and busied himself with his canoe, as though he were afraid that the Doctor might again ask him to paddle him to the island.

"Look here, Jip," said John Dolittle, "you said you got this bone from No-Man's-Land. Did you see any dragons there?"

"No," said Jip. "I swam out there—just to get cool. It was a hot day yesterday. And then I didn't go far inland on the island. I found many bones on the beach. And as this one smelled good to me, I picked it up and swam back here with it. I was more interested in the bone and the swim than I was in the island, to tell you the truth."

"It's most extraordinary," murmured the Doctor, "this legend about the island. It makes me more anxious than ever to go there. That bone interests me, too, immensely. I've seen only one other like it—and that was in a natural-history museum. Do you mind if I keep it, Jip? I'd like to put it in my own museum when I get back to Puddleby."

"Not at all," said Jip. "Look here, Doctor, if we can't raise a canoe, let's you and I swim out to the island. It's not over a mile and a half and we're both good swimmers."

"That's not a bad idea, Jip," said the Doctor. "We'll go down the shore a way till we're opposite the island; then we won't have so far to swim."

So off they went. And when they had come to the best place on the shore, the Doctor took off his clothes and, tying them up in a bundle, he fastened them on his head, with the precious high hat on the top of all. Then he waded into the surf and, with Jip beside him, started swimming for the island.

Now this particular stretch of water they were trying to cross happened to be a bad place for swimming. And after about a quarter of an hour Jip and the Doctor felt themselves being carried out to sea in the grip of a powerful current. They tried their hardest to get to the island. But without any success.

"Let yourself drift, Doctor," panted Jip. "Don't waste your strength fighting the current. Let yourself drift. Even if we're carried past the island out to sea we can land on the mainland farther down the coast, where the current isn't so strong."

But the Doctor didn't answer. And Jip could see from his face that his strength and breath were nearly gone.

Then Jip barked his loudest, hoping that possibly Dab-Dab might hear him on the mainland and fly out and bring help. But, of course, they were much too far from the town for anyone to hear.

"Turn back, Jip," gasped the Doctor. "Don't bother about me. I'll be all right. Turn back and try and make the shore."

But Jip had no intention of turning back and leaving the Doctor to drown—though he saw no possible chance of rescue.

Presently John Dolittle's mouth filled with water and he began to splutter and gurgle and Jip was really frightened. But just as the Doctor's eyes were closing and he seemed too weak to swim another stroke, a curious thing happened. Jip felt something come up under the water, right beneath his feet, and lift him and the Doctor slowly out of the sea, like the rising deck of a submarine. Up and up they were lifted, now entirely out of the water. And, gasping and sprawling side by side, they gazed at each other in utter astonishment.

"What is it, Doctor?" said Jip, staring down at the strange

HUGH LOFTING

" 'Turn back, Jip!' gasped the Doctor"

thing, which had now stopped rising and was carrying them like a ship, right across the strong course of the current, in the direction of the island.

"I haven't the—hah—remotest—hah—idea," panted John Dolittle. "Can it be a whale? No, because the skin isn't a whale's. This is fur," he said, plucking at the stuff he was sitting on.

"Well, it's an animal of some kind, isn't it?" said Jip. "But where's its head?" and he gazed down the long sloping back that stretched in a flat curve in front of them for a good thirty yards.

"Its head is under water," said the Doctor. "But there's its tail, look, behind us."

And turning around Jip saw the longest tail that mortal beast ever had, thrashing the water and driving them toward the island.

"I know!" cried Jip. "It's the dragon! This is King Kakaboochi's mother-in-law we're sitting on!"

"Well, anyway, thank goodness she rose in time!" said the Doctor, shaking the water out of his ears. "I was never so near drowning in my life. I suppose I'd better make myself a little more presentable before she gets her head out of water."

And, taking down his clothes off his own head, the Doctor smartened up his high hat and dressed himself, while the strange thing that had saved their lives carried them steadily and firmly toward the mysterious island.

· Chapter 7 ·

THE ANIMALS' PARADISE

At length the extraordinary creature that had come to their rescue reached the island; and with Jip and the Doctor still clinging to his wide back, he crawled out of the water on to the beach.

And then John Dolittle, seeing its head for the first time, cried out in great excitement, "Jip, it's a quiffenodochus, as sure as I'm alive!"

"A quiffeno-what-us?" asked Jip.

"A quiffenodochus," said the Doctor. "A prehistoric beast! Naturalists thought they were extinct—that there weren't any more live ones anywhere in the world. This is a great day, Jip. I'm awfully glad I came here."

The tremendous animal which the Fantippans had called a dragon had now climbed right up the beach and was standing fully revealed in all his strangeness. At first he looked like some curious mixture between a crocodile and a giraffe. He had short, spreading legs but an enormously long tail and neck. On his head were two stubby little horns.

As soon as the Doctor and Jip had climbed down off his back he swung his head around on the end of that enormous neck and said to the Doctor, "Do you feel all right now?"

"Yes, thanks," said John Dolittle.

"I was afraid," said the creature, "that I wouldn't be in time to save your life. It was my brother who first saw you. We thought it was a native and we were getting ready to give him our usual terrifying reception. But while we watched from behind the trees my brother suddenly cried, 'Great heavens! That's Doctor Dolittle—and he's drowning. See, how he waves his arms! He must be saved at any cost. There isn't one man like that born in a thousand years! Let's go after him, quick!' Then word was passed around the island that John Dolittle, the great doctor, was drowning out in the straits. Of course, we had all heard of you. And, rushing down to a secret cove that we have on the far side of the island, we dashed into the sea and swam out to you under water. I was the best swimmer and got to you first. I'm awfully glad I was in time. You're sure you feel all right?"

"Oh, quite," said the Doctor, "thank you. But why did you swim under water?"

"We didn't want the natives to see us," said the strange beast. "They think we are dragons—and we let them go on thinking it. Because then they don't come near the island and we have our country to ourselves."

The creature stretched his long neck still longer and whispered in the Doctor's ear, "They think we live on men and breathe fire! But all we ever really eat is bananas. And when anyone tries to come here we go down to a hollow in the middle of the island and suck up the mist, the fog, that

" 'All we eat is bananas' "

always hangs around there. Then we come back to the beach and roar and rampage. And we breathe the fog out through our nostrils and they think it's smoke. That's the way we've kept this island to ourselves for a thousand years. And this is the only part of the world where we are left—where we can live in peace."

"How very interesting!" said the Doctor. "Naturalists have thought your kind of animals are no longer living, you know. You are quiffenodochi, are you not?"

"Oh, no," said the beast. "The quiffenodochus has gone long ago. We are the piffilosaurus. We have six toes on the back feet, while the quiffenodochi, our cousins, have only five. They died out about two thousand years ago."

"But where are the rest of your people?" asked the Doctor. "I thought you said that many of you had swum out to rescue us."

"They did," said the piffilosaurus. "But they kept hidden under the water, lest the natives on the shore should see and get to know that the old story about the King's mother-in-law wasn't true. While I was bringing you here they were swimming all around you under the water, ready to help if I needed them. They have gone around to the secret cove so they may come ashore unseen. We had better be going on ourselves now. Whatever happens, we mustn't be seen from the shore and have the natives coming here. It would be the end of us if that should ever happen because, between ourselves, although they think us so terrible, we are really more harmless than sheep."

"Do any other animals live here?" asked the Doctor.

"Oh, yes, indeed," said the piffilosaurus. "This island is entirely peopled by harmless, vegetable-feeding creatures. If we had the others, of course, we wouldn't last long. But come, I will show you around the island. Let us go quietly up that valley there, so we shan't be seen till we reach the cover of the woods."

Then John Dolittle and Jip were taken by the piffilosaurus all over the island of No-Man's-Land.

The Doctor said afterward that he had never had a more enjoyable or more instructive day. The shores of the island all around were high and steep, which gave it the appearance Jip had spoken of—like a plum pudding. But in the center, on top, there was a deep and pleasant hollow, invisible from the sea and sheltered from the winds. In this great bowl, a good thirty miles across, the piffilosauruses had lived at peace for a thousand years, eating ripe bananas and frolicking in the sun.

Down by the banks of the streams the Doctor was shown great herds of hippopotami, feeding on the luscious reeds that grew at the water's edge. In the wide fields of high grass there were elephants and rhinoceri browsing. On the slopes where the forests were sparse he spied long-necked giraffes, nibbling from the trees. Monkeys and deer of all kinds were plentiful. And birds swarmed everywhere.

Standing on the top of the hill with Jip and the piffilosaurus at his side, the Doctor gazed down over the wide bowl full of contented animal life and heaved a sigh.

"This beautiful land could also have been called the 'Animals' Paradise,'" he murmured. "Long may they enjoy it to themselves! May this, indeed, be *No-Man's-Land* forever!"

"You, Doctor," said the deep voice of the piffilosaurus at his elbow, "are the first human in a thousand years that has set foot here. The last one was King Kakaboochi's mother-in-law."

"By the way, what really became of her?" asked the Doctor. "The natives believe she was turned into a dragon, you know."

"We married her off," said the great creature, nibbling idly at a lily stalk. "We couldn't stand her here, any more than the King could. You never heard anybody talk so in all your life. Yes, we carried her one dark night by sea far down the coast of Africa and left her at the palace door of a deaf king, who ruled over a small country south of the

Congo River. He married her. Of course, being deaf, he didn't mind her everlasting chatter in the least."

And now for several days the Doctor forgot all about his post-office work and King Koko and his ship at anchor, and everything else. For he was kept busy from morning to night with all the animals who wanted to consult him about different things.

Many of the giraffes were suffering from sore hoofs, and he showed them where to find a special root that could be put into a foot bath and would bring immediate relief. The rhinoceroses' horns were growing too long, and John Dolittle explained to them how, by grinding them against a certain kind of stone and by eating less grass and more berries, they could keep the growth down. A special sort of nut tree that the deer were fond of had grown scarce and almost died out from constant nibbling. And the Doctor showed the chief stags how, by taking a few nuts and poking them down into the soft earth with their hoofs before the rainy season set in, they could make new trees grow and so increase the supply.

One day when he was pulling out a loose tooth for a baby hippopotamus with his watch chain, Speedy-the-Skimmer turned up, looking rather annoyed.

"Well," said the neat little bird, settling down on the ground at his feet, "I've found you at last, Doctor. I've been hunting all over creation for you."

"Oh, hulloa, Speedy," said the Doctor. "Glad to see you. Did you want me for something?"

"Why, of course I did," said Speedy. "We finished the nesting season two days ago, and you had said you wanted to see me about some special business as soon as it was over. I went to your house, but Dab-Dab had no idea where

"He was pulling out a loose tooth"

you could be. Then I hunted all over. At last I heard some
gossiping boatmen down at the harbor say that you came
to this island five days ago and had never returned. All the
Fantippans have given you up for lost. They say you have
surely been eaten by the dragons that live here. I got an
awful fright—though, of course, *I* didn't quite believe the
dragon story. Still, you had been gone so long I didn't
know what to make of it. The post office, as you can imagine, is in a worse mess than ever."

"Humph!" said the Doctor, who had now gotten the loose tooth out and was showing the baby hippo how to rinse his mouth in the river. "I'm sorry. I suppose I should have sent you a message. But I've been so awfully busy. Let's go up under the shade of those palms and sit down. It was about the post office that I wanted to talk to you."

· Chapter 8 ·
THE SWIFTEST MAIL
IN THE WORLD

So the Doctor and Jip and Speedy-the-Skimmer sat down in the shade of the palm trees and for the first time plans for that great service which was to be known as the Swallow Mail were discussed.

"Now, my idea, Speedy, is this," said the Doctor. "Regular foreign mails are difficult for the Fantippo post office because so few boats ever call there to bring or take the mails. Now, how would it be if you swallows did the letter carrying?"

"Well," said Speedy, "that would be possible. But, of course, we could only do it during certain months of the year when we were in Africa. And then we could only take letters to the mild and warm countries. We should get frozen if we had to carry mail where severe winters were going on."

"Oh, of course," said the Doctor. "I wouldn't expect you to do that. But I had thought we might get the other birds to help—cold-climate birds, hot-climate ones, and temperate. And if some of the trips were too far or disagreeable for one kind of birds to make, we could deliver the mail in

"They sat down in the shade of a palm tree"

relays. I mean, for instance, a letter going from here to the North Pole could be carried by the swallows as far as the north end of Africa. From there it would be taken by thrushes up to the top of Scotland. There seagulls would take it from the thrushes and carry it as far as Greenland. And from there penguins would take it to the north pole. What do you think?"

"I think it might be all right," said Speedy, "if we can get the other birds to go in with us on the idea."

"Well, you see," said John Dolittle, "I think we might because we could use the mail service for the birds themselves, and the animals, too, to send their letters by, as well as the Fantippans."

"But, Doctor, birds and animals don't send letters," said Speedy.

"No," said the Doctor. "But there's no reason why they shouldn't begin. Neither did people write nor send letters once upon a time. But as soon as they began they found it very useful and convenient. So would the birds and animals. We could have the head office here in this beautiful island—in this Animals' Paradise. You see, my idea is, firstly, a post-office system for the education and betterment of the animal kingdom, and, secondly, a good foreign mail for the Fantippans. Do you think we could ever find some way by which birds could write letters?"

"Oh, yes, I think so," said Speedy. "We swallows, for instance, always leave marks on houses where we have nested that are messages for those who may come after us. Look"—Speedy scratched some crosses and signs in the sand at the Doctor's feet—"that means *Don't build your nest in this house. They have a cat here!* And this"—the Skimmer made four more signs in the sand—"this means *Good house. Flies plentiful. Folks quiet. Building mud can be found behind the stable.*'"

"Splendid," cried the Doctor. "It's a kind of shorthand. You say a whole sentence in four signs."

"And, then," Speedy went on, "nearly all other kinds of birds have a sign language of their own. For example, the kingfishers have a way of marking the trees along the river to show where good fishing is to be found. And thrushes have signs, too; one I've often seen on stones, which means

'*Crack your snail shells here.*' That's so the thrushes won't go throwing their snail shells all over the place and scare the live snails into keeping out of sight."

"There you are," said the Doctor. "I always thought you birds had at least the beginnings of a written language—otherwise you couldn't be so clever. Now all we have to do is to build up on these signs a regular and proper system of bird-writing. And I have no doubt whatever that with the animals we can do the same thing. Then we'll get the Swallow Mail going and we'll have animals and birds writing letters to one another all over the world—and to people, too, if they want to."

"I suspect," said Speedy, "that you'll find most of the letters will be written to you, Doctor. I've met birds all over creation who wanted to know what you looked like, what you ate for breakfast, and all sorts of silly things about you."

"Well," said the Doctor. "I won't mind that. But my idea is firstly an educational one. With a good post-office system of their own, I feel that the condition of the birds and animals will be greatly bettered. Only today, for example, some deer on this very island asked me what they should do about their nut trees, which were nearly eaten up. I showed them at once how they could plant seeds and grow more trees. Heaven knows how long they had been going on short rations. But if they'd only been able to write to me, I could have told them long ago—by Swallow Mail."

Then the Doctor and Jip went back to Fantippo, carried by the piffilosaurus, who landed them on the shore under cover of night, so no one would see them. And in the morning John Dolittle called upon the King again.

"Your Majesty," said the Doctor, "I have now a plan to

provide your country with an excellent service of foreign mails if you will agree to what I suggest."

"Good," said the King. "My Majesty is listening. Proceed. Let me offer you a lollipop."

The Doctor took one—a green one—from the box the King held out to him. King Koko was very proud of the quality of his lollipops—made in the Royal Candy Kitchen. He was never without one himself, and always wore it hung around his neck on a ribbon. But constant lollipops had ruined his figure and made him dreadfully stout. However, as fatness was considered a sign of greatness in Fantippo, he didn't mind that.

"My plan," said the Doctor, "is this: The domestic mails of Fantippo, after I have instructed the postmen a little more, can be carried by your own people. But the handling of foreign mails as well as the domestic ones is too much for them. And, besides, you have so few boats calling at your port. So I propose to build a floating post office for the foreign mails that shall be anchored close to the island called"—the Doctor only just stopped himself in time from speaking the dreaded name— "er—er—close to the island I spoke of to you the other day."

"I don't like that," said the King, frowning.

"Your Majesty need have no fear," the Doctor put in hurriedly. "It will never be necessary for any of your people to land upon the island. The foreign-mail post office will be a houseboat anchored a little way out from the shore. And I will not need any Fantippan postmen to run it at all. On the contrary, I make it a special condition on your part that—er—the island we are speaking of shall continue to be left undisturbed for all time. I am going to run the foreign-mails office in my own way—with special postmen of my own. When the Fantippans wish to send out letters to foreign lands they must come by canoe and bring them to the houseboat post office. But incoming letters addressed to the people in Fantippo shall be delivered at the doors of the houses in the regular way. What do you say to that?"

"I agree," said the King. "But the stamps must all have my beautiful face upon them, and no other."

"Very good," said the Doctor. "That can be arranged. But it must be clearly understood that from now on the foreign mails shall be handled by my own postmen—in *my* way. And after I have got the domestic post office running properly in Fantippo you must see to it that it continues to work in order. If you will do that in a few weeks' time I think I can promise that your kingdom shall have the finest mail service in the world."

Then the Doctor asked Speedy to send off messages through the birds to every corner of the earth. And to ask all the leaders of sea gulls, tomtits, magpies, thrushes, stormy petrels, finches, penguins, vultures, snow buntings, wild geese, and the rest to come to No-Man's-Land because John Dolittle wanted to speak to them.

So the good Speedy sent off messengers; and all around the world and back again, word was passed from bird to bird that John Dolittle, the famous animal doctor, wished to see all the leaders of all kinds of birds, great and small.

And presently in the big hollow in the center of No-Man's-Land they began to arrive. After three days Speedy came to the Doctor and said, "All right, Doctor, they are ready for you now."

A good strong canoe had by this time been put at the Doctor's service by the King, who was also having the post-office houseboat built at the Doctor's orders.

So John Dolittle got into his canoe and came at length to the same hill where he had before gazed out over the pleasant hollow of the Animals' Paradise. And with the Skimmer on his shoulder he looked down into a great sea of bird faces—leaders all—every kind, from a hummingbird to an albatross. And taking a palm leaf and twisting it into a trumpet, so that he could make himself heard, he began his great inauguration speech to the leaders which was to set working the famous Swallow Mail Service.

After the Doctor had finished his speech, the birds of the world applauded by whistling and screeching and flapping their wings, so that the noise was terrible. And in the streets of Fantippo the natives whispered it about that the dragons were fighting one another in No-Man's-Land.

Then the Doctor spoke to each bird leader in turn, asking him questions about the signs and sign language that his particular kind of bird was in the habit of using. The Doctor wrote it all down in his notebook and took it home with him.

And on the morrow, he went on with the discussions. It was agreed that the head office should be here in No-Man's-Land. And that there should be branch offices at Cape Horn, Greenland, in Christmas Island, Tahiti, Kashmir, Tibet and Puddleby-on-the-Marsh. Most of the mails were arranged so that those birds who migrated or went to other lands in the winter and back again in summer should carry the letters on their regular yearly journeys. And as there are some kinds of birds crossing from one land to another in almost every week of the year, this took care of much of the mails without difficulty.

Then there were those birds who don't leave their homelands in winter, but stay in one country all the time. The

HUGH LOFTING

"He began his great inauguration speech"

leaders of these had come under special guidance of other
birds to oblige the Doctor by being present at the great
meeting. They promised to have their people all the year
round take care of letters that were brought to their particular countries to be delivered.

Then the Doctor and the leaders agreed upon a regular
kind of simple, easy writing for all birds to use, so that the
addresses on the envelopes could be understood and read
by the postbirds. And at last John Dolittle sent them off

home again, to instruct their relatives in this new writing and reading and explain how the post office was going to work and how much good he hoped it would do for the animal kingdom. Then he went home and had a good sleep.

The next morning he found that King Koko had gotten his post-office houseboat ready and finished. It was paddled out and anchored close to the shore of the island. Then Dab-Dab, Jip, Too-Too, Gub-Gub, the pushmi-pullyu, and the white mouse were brought over, and the Doctor gave up his house on the main street of Fantippo and settled down to live at the foreign-mails post office for the remainder of his stay.

And now John Dolittle and his animals got tremendously busy arranging the post office, its furniture, the stamp drawers, the postcard drawers, the weighing scales, the sorting bags, and all the rest of the paraphernalia. Dab-Dab, of course, was housekeeper, as usual, and she saw to it that the post office was swept properly every morning. Jip was the watchman and had charge of locking up at night and opening in the morning. Too-Too, with his head for mathematics, was given the bookkeeping, and he kept an account of how many stamps were sold and how much money was taken in. The Doctor ran the information window and answered the hundred and one questions that people are always asking at post offices. And the good and trusty Speedy was here, there, and everywhere.

And this was how the first letter was sent off by the Swallow Mail: King Koko himself came one morning and, putting his large face in at the information window, asked, "What is the fastest foreign mail delivery ever made by any post office anywhere in the world?"

"The British post office is now boasting," said the Doctor, "that it can get a letter from London to Canada in fourteen days."

"All right," said the King. "Here's a letter to a friend of mine who runs a shoe-shine parlor in Alabama. Let me see how quickly you can get me an answer to it."

Now, the Doctor really had not gotten everything ready yet to work the foreign mails properly and he was about to explain to the King.

But Speedy hopped up on the desk and whispered, "Give me that letter, Doctor. We'll show him."

Then going outside, he called for Quip the Carrier. "Quip," said Speedy, "take this letter to the Azores as fast as you can. There you'll just catch the white-tailed Carolina warblers about to make their summer crossing to the United States. Give it to them and tell them to get the answer back here as quick as they know how."

In a flash Quip was gone, seaward.

It was four o'clock in the afternoon when the King brought that letter to the Doctor. And when His Majesty woke up in the morning and came down to breakfast, there was the answer to it lying beside his plate!

PART TWO

· Chapter 1 ·
A MOST UNUSUAL POST OFFICE

Certainly in the whole history of the world there never was another post office like the Doctor's. For one thing, it was a houseboat post office; for another, tea was served to everybody—the clerks and the customers as well—regularly at four o'clock every afternoon, with cucumber sandwiches on Sundays. Paddling over to the foreign-mail post office for afternoon tea became quite the fashionable thing to do among the more up-to-date Fantippans. A large awning was put over the back entrance, forming a pleasant sort of veranda with a good view of the ocean and the bay. And if you dropped in for a stamp around four o'clock, as likely as not you would meet the King there, and all the other high notables of Fantippo, sipping tea.

Another thing in which the Doctor's post office was different from others was the gum used on the stamps. The supply of gum that the King had been using for his stamps ran short, and the Doctor had to set about discovering and making a new kind. And after a good deal of experiment

"The houseboat post office of No-Man's-Land"

he invented a gum made of licorice, which dried quickly and worked very well. But, as I have said, the Fantippans were very fond of sweets. And soon after the new gum was put into use, the post office was crowded with people buying stamps by the hundred.

At first the Doctor could not understand this sudden new rush of business—which kept Too-Too, the cashier, working overtime every night, adding up the day's takings. The post-office safe could hardly hold all the money taken in, and the overflow had to be put in a vase on the kitchen mantelpiece.

But presently the Doctor noticed that after they had licked the gum off the stamps, the customers would bring them back and want to exchange them for money again. So the Doctor saw that he would have to change his kind of gum if he wanted to keep stamps that would stick.

And one day the King's brother came to the post office with a terrible cough and asked him in the same breath (or gasp) to give him five halfpenny stamps and a cure for a cough. This gave the Doctor an idea. And the next gum that he invented for his stamps he called *whooping-cough gum.* He made it out of a special kind of sweet, sticky cough mixture. He also invented a *bronchitis gum,* a *mumps gum,* and several others. And whenever there was a catching disease in the town the Doctor would see that the proper kind of gum to cure it was issued on the stamps. It saved him a lot of trouble because the people were always bothering him to cure colds and sore throats and things. And he was the first postmaster general to use this way of getting rid of sickness—by serving around pleasant medicine on the backs of stamps. He called it *stamping out* an epidemic.

One evening at six o'clock Jip shut the doors of the post office as usual, and hung up the sign *"Closed"* as he always did at that hour. The Doctor heard the bolts being shot and he stopped counting postcards and took out his pipe to have a smoke.

The first hard work of getting the post office in full swing was now over. And that night John Dolittle felt when he heard the doors being shut that at last he could afford to

"Jip hung up the sign"

keep more regular hours and not be working all the time. And when Jip came inside the registered-mail booth he found the Doctor leaning back in a chair, with his feet on the desk, gazing around him with great satisfaction.

"Well, Jip," said he with a sigh, "we now have a real working post office."

"Yes," said Jip, putting down his watchman's lantern, "and a mighty good one it is, too. There isn't another like it anywhere."

"You know," said John Dolittle, "although we opened more than a week ago I haven't myself written a single letter yet. Fancy living in a post office for a week and never writing a letter! Look at that drawer there. Ordinarily the sight of so many stamps would make me write dozens of letters. All my life I never had a stamp when I really wanted to write a letter. And—funny thing!—now that I'm living and sleeping in a post office, I can't think of a single person to write to."

"It's a shame," said Jip. "And you with such beautiful handwriting, too—as well as a drawerful of stamps! Never mind. Think of all the animals that are waiting to hear from you."

"Of course, there's Sarah," the Doctor went on puffing at his pipe dreamily. "Poor, dear Sarah! I wonder whom she married. But there you are, I haven't her address. So I can't write to Sarah. And I don't suppose any of my old patients would want to hear from me."

"I know!" cried Jip. "Write to the cat's-meat man."

"He can't read," said the Doctor gloomily.

"No, but his wife can," said Jip.

"That's true," murmured the Doctor. "But what shall I write to him about?"

Just at that moment Speedy-the-Skimmer came in and said, "Doctor, we've got to do something about the city deliveries in Fantippo. My postbirds are not very good at finding the right houses to deliver the letters. You see we swallows, although we nest in houses, are not regular city birds. We pick out lonely houses, as a rule—in the country. City streets are a bit difficult for swallows to find their way around in. Some of the postbirds have brought back the letters they took out this morning to deliver, saying they can't find the houses they are addressed to."

"Humph!" said the Doctor. "That's too bad. Let me think a minute. Oh, I know! I'll send for Cheapside."

"Who is Cheapside?" asked Speedy.

"Cheapside is a London sparrow," said the Doctor, "who visits me every summer in Puddleby. The rest of the year he lives around St. Paul's Cathedral. He builds his nest in St. Edmund's left ear."

"*Where?*" cried Jip.

"In the left ear of a statue of St. Edmund on the outside of the chancel—the cathedral, you know," the Doctor explained. "Cheapside's the very fellow we want for city deliveries. There's nothing about houses and towns he doesn't know. I'll send for him right away."

"I'm afraid," said Speedy, "that a postbird—unless he was a city bird himself—would have a hard job finding a sparrow in London. It's an awful big city, isn't it?"

"Yes, that's so," said John Dolittle.

"Listen, Doctor," said Jip. "You were wondering just now what to write the cat's-meat man about. Let Speedy write the letter to Cheapside in bird scribble and you enclose it in a letter to the cat's-meat man. Then when the sparrow comes to Puddleby for his summer visit, the cat's-meat man can give it to him."

"Splendid!" cried the Doctor. And he snatched a piece of paper off the desk and started to write.

"And you might ask him too," put in Dab-Dab, who had been listening, "to take a look at the back windows of the house to see that none of them is broken. We don't want the rain coming in on the beds."

"All right," said the Doctor. "I'll mention that."

So the Doctor's letter was written and addressed to *Matthew Mugg, Esquire, Cat's-Meat Merchant, Puddleby-on-the-Marsh, Slopshire, England.* And it was sent off by Quip-the-Carrier.

The Doctor did not expect an answer to it right away because the cat's-meat man's wife was a very slow reader and a still slower writer. And anyhow, Cheapside could not be expected to visit Puddleby for another week yet. He always stayed in London until after the Easter Bank Holiday. His wife refused to let him leave for the country till the spring family had been taught by their father how to find the houses where people threw out crumbs; how to pick up oats from under the cab horses' nose bags without being stamped on by the horses' hoofs; how to get about in the trafficky streets of London; and a whole lot of other things that young city birds have to know.

While Quip was gone, life went forward busily and happily at the Doctor's post office. The animals—Too-Too, Dab-Dab, Gub-Gub, the pushmi-pullyu, the white mouse, and Jip—all agreed that they found living in a houseboat post office great fun. Whenever they got tired of their floating home they would go off for picnic parties to the island of No-Man's-Land, which was now more often called by the name John Dolittle had given it, the "Animals' Paradise."

On these trips too, the Doctor sometimes accompanied them. He was glad to, because he so got an opportunity of talking with the many different kinds of animals there about the signs they were in the habit of using. And on these signs, which he carefully put down in notebooks, he built up a sort of written language for animals to use—or *animal scribble,* as he called it—the same as he had done with the birds.

"He held scribbling classes for the animals"

Whenever he could spare the time he held afternoon scribbling classes for the animals in the Great Hollow. And they were very well attended. He found the monkeys, of course, the easiest to teach and, because they were so clever, he made some of them into assistant teachers. But the zebras were quite bright too. The Doctor discovered that these intelligent beasts had ways of marking and twisting the grasses to show where they had smelled lions about—though, happily, they did not have to use this trick in the Animals' Paradise but had brought it with them when they had swum across from the mainland of Africa.

The Doctor's pets found it quite thrilling to go through the mail that arrived each day to see if there were any letters for them. At the beginning of course there wasn't much. But one day Quip had returned from Puddleby with an answer to the Doctor's letter to the cat's-meat man. Mr. Matthew Mugg had written (through his wife) that he had hung the letter for Cheapside on an apple tree in the garden, where the sparrow would surely see it when he arrived. The windows of the house were all right, he wrote; but the back door could do with a coat of paint.

And while Quip had been waiting for this letter to be written he had filled in the time at Puddleby by gossiping with all the starlings and blackbirds in the Doctor's garden about the wonderful new animals' post office on the island of No-Man's-Land. And pretty soon every creature in and around Puddleby had gotten to hear of it.

After that, of course, letters began to arrive at the house-boat for the Doctor's pets. And one morning, when the mail was sorted, there was a letter for Dab-Dab from her sister; one for the white mouse written by a cousin from the Doctor's bureau drawer; one for Jip from the collie who lived next door in Puddleby; and one for Too-Too, telling him he had a new family of six young ones in the rafters of the stable. But there was nothing for Gub-Gub. The poor pig was nearly in tears at being left out. And when the Doctor went into town that afternoon, Gub-Gub asked could he come along.

The next day the postbirds complained that the mail was an extra-heavy one. And when it was sorted, there were ten thick letters for Gub-Gub and none for anybody else. Jip got suspicious about this and looked over Gub-Gub's shoulder while he opened them. In each one there was a banana skin.

"Who sent you those?" asked Jip.

"I sent them to myself," said Gub-Gub, "from Fantippo yesterday. I don't see why you fellows should get all the mail. Nobody writes to me, so I write to myself."

· Chapter 2 ·

CHEAPSIDE

It was a great day at the Doctor's post office when Cheapside, the London sparrow, arrived from Puddleby to look after the city deliveries for Fantippo.

The Doctor was eating his lunch of sandwiches at the information desk when the little bird popped his head through the window and said in his cheeky cockney voice, " 'Ulloa, Doctor, 'ere we are again! What ho! The old firm! Who would 'ave thought you'd come to this?"

Cheapside was a character. Anyone on seeing him for the first time would probably guess that he spent his life in city streets. His whole expression was different from other birds. In Speedy's eyes, for instance—though nobody would dream of thinking him stupid—there was an almost noble look of country honesty. But in the eyes of Cheapside, the London sparrow, there was a saucy, daredevil expression that seemed to say "Don't you think for one moment that you'll ever get the better of me. I'm a cockney bird."

"Cheapside, the London sparrow"

"Why, Cheapside!" cried John Dolittle. "At last you've come. My, but it's good to see you! Did you have a pleasant journey?"

"Not bad—not 'alf bad," said Cheapside, eyeing some crumbs from the Doctor's lunch that lay upon the desk. "No storms. Pretty decent travelin'. 'Ot? Well, I should say it *was* 'ot. 'Ot enough for an 'Ottentot! . . . Quaint place you 'ave 'ere—sort of a barge?"

By this time all the animals had heard Cheapside

arriving and they came rushing in to see the traveler and to hear the news of Puddleby and England.

"How is the old horse in the stable?" asked John Dolittle.

"Pretty spry," said Cheapside. "Course 'e ain't as young as 'e used to be. But 'e's lively enough for an old 'un. 'E asked me to bring you a bunch of crimson ramblers—just bloomin' over the stable door, they was. But I says to 'im, I says, 'What d'yer take me for, an omnibus?' Fancy a feller at my time of life carrying a bunch of roses all the way down the Atlantic! Folks would think I was goin' to a weddin' at the south pole."

"Gracious, Cheapside!" said the Doctor, laughing. "It makes me quite homesick for England to hear your cockney chirp."

"And me, too," sighed Jip. "Were there many rats in the woodshed, Cheapside?"

"'Undreds of them," said the sparrow. "As big as rabbits. And that uppish you'd think they owned the place!"

"I'll soon settle *them*, when I get back," said Jip. "I hope we go soon."

"How does the garden look, Cheapside?" asked the Doctor.

"A1," said the sparrow. "Weeds in the paths, o' course. But the iris under the kitchen window looked something lovely, they did."

"Anything new in London?" asked the white mouse, who was also city-bred.

"Yes," said Cheapside. "There's always something doing in good old London. They've got a new kind of cab that goes on two wheels instead of four. A man called 'Ansom invented it. Much faster than the old 'ackneys, they are.

You see 'em everywhere. And there's a new greengrocer's shop near the Royal Exchange."

"I'm going to have a greengrocer's shop of my own when I grow up," murmured Gub-Gub, "In England where they grow good vegetables—I'm awfully tired of Africa—and then I'll watch the new vegetables coming into season all year round."

"He's always talking about that," said Too-Too. "Such an ambition in life to have—to run a greengrocer's shop!"

"Ah, England!" cried Gub-Gub sentimentally. "What is there more beautiful in life than the heart of a young lettuce in the spring?"

"'Ark at 'im," said Cheapside, raising his eyebrows. "Ain't 'e the poetical porker? Why don't you write a bunch of sonnets to the skunk-kissed cabbages of Louisiana, Mr. Bacon?"

"Well, now, look here, Cheapside," said the Doctor. "We want you to get these city deliveries straightened out for us in the town of Fantippo. Our postbirds are having great difficulty finding the right houses to take letters to. You're a city bird, born and bred. Do you think you can help us?"

"I'll see what I can do for you, Doc," said the sparrow, "after I've taken a look around this 'eathen town of yours. But first I want a bath. I'm all heat up from flying under a broiling sun. Ain't you got no puddles around here for a bird to take a bath in?"

"No, this isn't puddly climate," said the Doctor. "You're not in England, you know. But I'll bring you my shaving mug and you can take a bath in that."

"Mind, you wash the soap out first, Doc," chirped the sparrow, "it gets into my eyes."

The next day after Cheapside had had a good sleep to

rest up from his long journey, the Doctor took the London sparrow to show him around the town of Fantippo.

"Well, Doc," said Cheapside after they had seen the sights, "as a town I don't think much of it—really, I don't. It's big. I'll say that for it. I 'ad no idea they 'ad towns as big as this in Africa. But the streets is so narrow! I can see why they don't 'ave no cabs 'ere—'ardly room for a goat to pass, let alone a four-wheeler. And as for the 'ouses, they seem to be made of the insides of old mattresses. The first thing we'll 'ave to do is to make old King Coconut tell 'is subjects to put door knockers on their doors. What is 'ome without a door knocker, I'd like to know? Of course, your postmen can't deliver the letters, when they've no knockers to knock with."

"I'll attend to that," said the Doctor. "I'll see the King about it this afternoon."

"And then, they've got no letter boxes in the doors," said Cheapside. "There ought to be slots made to poke the letters in. The only place these bloomin' 'eathens have for a postman to put a letter is down the chimney."

"Very well," said the Doctor. "I'll attend to that, too. Shall I have the letter boxes in the middle of the door, or would you like them on one side?"

"Put 'em on each side of the doors—two to every 'ouse," said Cheapside.

"What's that for?" asked the Doctor.

"That's a little idea of my own," said the sparrow. "We'll 'ave one box for the bills and one for sure-enough letters. You see, people are so disappointed when they 'ear the postman's knock and come to the door, expecting to find a nice letter from a friend or news that money's been left them and all they get is a bill from the tailor. But if we have two boxes on each door, one marked *'Bills,'* and the other *'Letters,'* the postman can put all the bills in one box and the honest letters in the other. As I said, it's a little idea of my own. We might as well be real up-to-date. What do you think of it?"

"I think it's a splendid notion," said the Doctor. "Then the people need only have one disappointment—when they clear the bill box on the day set for paying their debts."

"That's the idea," said Cheapside. "And tell the postbirds —as soon as we've got the knockers on—to knock once for a bill and twice for a letter, so the folks in the 'ouse will know whether to come and get the mail or not. We'll 'ave a post office in Fantipsy that really is a post office. And, now, 'ow about the Christmas boxes, Doctor? Postmen always expect a handsome present around Christmastime, you know."

"Well, I'm rather afraid," said the Doctor doubtfully, "that these people don't celebrate Christmas as a holiday."

"Don't celebrate Christmas!" cried Cheapside in a shocked voice. "What a disgraceful scandal! Well, look here, Doctor. You just tell King Cocoa Butter that if 'e and 'is people don't celebrate the festive season by giving us postbirds Christmas boxes there ain't going to be no mail delivered in Fantipsy from New Year's to Easter. And you can tell 'im I said so. It's 'igh time somebody henlightened 'is hignorance."

"All right," said the Doctor, "I'll attend to that, too."

"Tell 'im," said Cheapside, "we'll expect two lumps of sugar on every doorstep Christmas morning for the postbirds. No sugar, no letters!"

That afternoon the Doctor called upon the King and explained to him the various things that Cheapside wanted.

And His Majesty gave in to them, every one. Beautiful brass knockers were screwed on all the doors—light ones, which the birds could easily lift. And very elegant they looked—by far the most up-to-date part of the ramshackle dwellings. The double boxes were also put up, with one place for bills and one for the letters.

John Dolittle instructed King Koko as well in the meaning of Christmastime, which should be a season for giving gifts. And among the Fantippo people the custom of making presents at Christmas became very general—not only to postmen, but to friends and relatives, too.

That is why when, several years after the Doctor had left this country, some missionaries visited that part of Africa, they found to their astonishment that Christmas was celebrated there. But they never learned that the custom had been brought about by Cheapside, the cheeky London sparrow.

And now very soon Cheapside took entire charge of the city delivery of mails in Fantippo. Of course, as soon as the mail began to get heavy, when the people got the habit of writing more to their friends and relatives, Cheapside could not deal with all the mail himself. So he sent a message by a swallow to get fifty sparrows from the streets of London (who were, like himself, accustomed to city ways), to help him with the delivery of letters. And around the native holiday seasons, the Harvest Moon and the Coming of the Rains, he had to send for fifty more to deal with the extra mail.

Cheapside's help was, indeed, most valuable to the Doctor. The King himself said that the mails were wonderfully managed. The letters were brought regularly and never left at the wrong house.

He had only one fault, had Cheapside. And that was being cheeky. Whenever he got into an argument his cockney swearing was just dreadful. And in spite of the Doctor's having issued orders time and time again that he expected his post-office clerks and mailbirds to be strictly polite to the public, Cheapside was always getting into rows—which he usually started himself.

One day when King Koko's pet white peacock came to the Doctor and complained that the cockney sparrow had made faces at him over the palace wall the Doctor became quite angry and read the city manager a long lecture.

Then Cheapside got together a gang of his tough London sparrow friends and one night they flew into the palace garden and mobbed the white peacock and pulled three feathers out of his beautiful tail.

This last piece of rowdyism was too much for John Dolittle and, calling up Cheapside, he discharged him on the spot—though he was very sorry to do it.

But when the sparrow went all his London friends went with him and the post office was left with no city birds to attend to the city deliveries. The swallows and other birds tried their hardest to get letters around to the houses properly. But they couldn't. And before long, complaints began to come in from the townspeople.

Then the Doctor was sorry and wished he hadn't discharged Cheapside, who seemed to be the only one who could manage this part of the mails properly.

But one day, to the Doctor's great delight—though he tried hard to look angry—Cheapside strolled into the post office with a straw in the corner of his mouth, looking as though nothing had happened.

John Dolittle had thought that he and his friends had

"The royal peacock complained that Cheapside
had made faces at him"

gone home to London. But they hadn't. They knew the
Doctor would need them, and they had just hung around
outside the town. And then the Doctor, after lecturing
Cheapside again about politeness, gave him back his job.

But the next day the rowdy little sparrow threw a bottle
of post-office ink over the royal white peacock when he
came to the houseboat with the King to take tea. Then the
Doctor discharged Cheapside again.

In fact, the Doctor used to discharge him for rudeness regularly about once a month. And the city mails always got tied up soon after. But, to the Doctor's great relief, the city manager always came back just when the tie-up was at its worst and put things right again.

Cheapside was a wonderful bird. But it seemed as though he just couldn't go a whole month without being rude to somebody. The Doctor said it was in his nature.

· Chapter 3 ·

CAPE STEPHEN LIGHT

On the coast of West Africa, about twenty miles to the northward of Fantippo, there was a cape running out into the sea that had a lighthouse on it called the Cape Stephen Light. This light was kept carefully burning by the government which controlled that part of Africa, in order that ships should see it from the sea and know where they were. It was a dangerous part of the coast, this. There were many rocks and shallows near the end of Cape Stephen. And if the light were ever allowed to go out at night, of course, ships traveling that part of the sea would be in great danger of running into the long cape and wrecking themselves.

Now, one evening the Doctor was writing letters in the post office by the light of a candle. It was late and all the animals were fast asleep long ago. Presently while he wrote he heard a sound a long way off, coming through the open window at his elbow. He put down his pen and listened.

It was the sound of a seabird, calling away out at sea.

"There were many rocks and shallows
near the end of Cape Stephen"

Now, seabirds don't, as a rule, call very much unless they
are in great numbers. This call sounded like a single bird.
The Doctor put his head through the window and looked
out.

It was a dark night, as black as pitch, and he couldn't see
a thing—especially as his eyes were used to the light of the
candle. The mysterious call was repeated again and again,
like a cry of distress from the sea. The Doctor didn't know

quite what to make of it. But soon he thought it seemed to be coming nearer. And, grabbing his hat, he ran out on to the veranda.

"What is it? What's the matter?" he shouted into the darkness over the sea.

He got no answer. But soon, with a rush of wings that nearly blew his candle out, a great seagull swept down on to the houseboat rail beside him.

"Doctor," panted the gull, "the Cape Stephen Light is out. I don't know what's the matter. It has never gone out before. We use it as a landmark, you know, when we are flying after dark. The night's as black as ink. I'm afraid some ship will surely run into the cape. I thought I'd come and tell you."

"Good heavens!" cried the Doctor. "What can have happened? There's a lighthouse keeper living there to attend to it. Was it lighted earlier in the evening?"

"I don't know," said the gull. "I was coming in from catching herring—they're running just now, you know, a little to the north. And, expecting to see the light, I lost my way and flew miles too far south. When I found out my mistake I went back, flying close down by the shore. And I came to Stephen Cape, but it had no light. It was black as anything. And I would have run right into the rocks myself if I hadn't been going carefully."

"How far would it be from here?" asked John Dolittle.

"Well, by land it would be twenty-five miles to where the lighthouse stands," said the gull. "But by water it would be only about twelve, I should say."

"All right," said the Doctor, hurrying into his coat. "Wait just a moment till I wake Dab-Dab."

The Doctor ran into the post-office kitchen and woke the

poor housekeeper, who was slumbering soundly beside the kitchen stove.

"Listen, Dab-Dab!" said the Doctor, shaking her. "Wake up! The Cape Stephen Light's gone out!"

"Whazhat?" said Dab-Dab, sleepily opening her eyes. "Stove's gone out?"

"No, the lighthouse on Cape Stephen," said the Doctor. "A gull just came and told me. The shipping's in danger. Wrecks, you know, and all that. Wake up and look sensible, for pity's sake!"

At last poor Dab-Dab, fully awakened, understood what was the matter. And in a moment she was up and doing.

"I know where it is, Doctor. I'll fly right over there—no, I won't need the gull to guide me. You keep him to show you the way. Follow me immediately in the canoe. If I can find out anything I'll come back and meet you halfway. If not, I'll wait for you by the lighthouse tower. Thank goodness, it's a calm night, anyway—even if it is dark!"

With a flap of her wings, Dab-Dab flew right through the open window and was gone into the night, while the Doctor grabbed his little black medicine bag and, calling to the gull to follow him, ran down to the other end of the houseboat, untied the canoe, and jumped in. Then he pushed off, headed around the island of No-Man's-Land and paddled for all he was worth for the seaward end of Cape Stephen.

About halfway to the long neck of land that jutted out into the gloomy ocean the Doctor's canoe was met by Dab-Dab—though how she found it in the darkness, with only the sound of the paddle to guide her, goodness only knows.

"Doctor," said she, "if the lighthouse keeper is in there at all he must be sick, or something. I hammered on the windows, but nobody answered."

"Dear me!" muttered the Doctor, paddling harder than ever, "I wonder what can have happened?"

"And that's not the worst," said Dab-Dab. "On the far side of the cape—you can't see it from here—there's the head-light of a big sailing ship, bearing down southward, making straight for the rocks. They can't see the lighthouse and they don't know what danger they're in."

"Good Lord!" groaned the Doctor, and he nearly broke the paddle as he churned the water astern to make the canoe go faster yet.

"How far off the rocks is the ship now?" asked the gull.

"About a mile, I should say," said Dab-Dab. "But she's a big one—judging by the height of her mast light—and she won't be long before she's aground on the cape."

"Keep right on, Doctor," said the gull. "I'm going off to get some friends of mine."

And the seagull spread his wings and flew away toward the land, calling the same cry as the Doctor had heard through the post-office window.

John Dolittle had no idea of what he meant to do. Nor was the gull himself sure that he would be in time to succeed with the plan he had in mind. But presently, to his delight, the seabird heard his call being answered from the rocky shores shrouded in darkness. And soon he had hundreds of his brother gulls circling round him in the night.

Then he took them to the great ship, which was sailing calmly onward toward the rocks and destruction. And there, going forward to where the helmsman held the spokes of the wheel and watched the compass swinging before him in the light of a little dim lamp, the gulls started dashing themselves into the wheelman's face and

HUGH LOFTING

"The gulls dashed themselves into the wheelman's face"

covering the glass of the compass, so he could not steer the ship.

The helmsman, battling with the birds, set up a yell for help, saying he couldn't see to steer the boat. Then the officers and sailors rushed up to his assistance and tried to beat the birds off.

In the meantime the Doctor, in his canoe, had reached the end of Cape Stephen and, springing ashore, he scrambled up the rocks to where the great tower of the lighthouse rose skyward over the black, unlighted sea. Feeling and fumbling, he found the door and hammered on it, yelling to be let in. But no one answered him. And Dab-Dab whispered in a hoarse voice that the light of the ship was nearer now—less than half a mile from the rocks.

Then the Doctor drew back for a run and threw his whole weight against the door. But the hinges and lock had been made to stand the beating of the sea, and they budged no more than if he had been a fly.

At last, with a roar of rage, the Doctor grabbed up a rock from the ground as big as a chair and banged it with all his might against the lock of the lighthouse door. With a crash the door flew open and the Doctor sprang within.

On the ship the seamen were still fighting with the gulls. The captain, seeing that no helmsman could steer the boat right with thousands of wings fluttering in his eyes, gave the orders to lay the ship to for a little and to get out the hose pipes. And a strong stream of water was turned onto the gulls around the helmsman, so they could no longer get near him. Then the ship got under way again and came on toward the cape once more.

Inside the lighthouse the Doctor found the darkness blacker still. With hands outstretched before him, he hurried forward, and the first thing he did was to stumble over a man who was lying on the floor just within the door. Without waiting to see what was the matter with him, the Doctor jumped over his body and began to grope his way up the winding stairs of the tower that led to the big lamp at the top.

Meanwhile Dab-Dab stayed below at the door, looking out over the sea at the mast light of the ship—which, after a short delay, was now coming on again toward the rocks.

At any minute she expected the great beam of the light-house lamp to flare out over the sea, as soon as the Doctor should get it lit, to warn the sailors of their danger. But, instead, she presently heard the Doctor's agonized voice calling from the head of the stairs:

"Dab-Dab! Dab-Dab! I can't light it. *We forgot to bring matches!*"

"Well, what have you *done* with the matches, Doctor?" called Dab-Dab. "They were always in your coat."

"I left them beside my pipe on the information desk," came the Doctor's voice from the top of the dark stairs. "But there must be matches in the lighthouse somewhere. We must find them."

"What chance have we of that?" shouted Dab-Dab. "It's as black as black down here. And the ship is coming nearer every minute."

"Feel in the man's pockets," called John Dolittle. "Hurry!"

In a minute Dab-Dab went through the pockets of the man who lay so still upon the floor.

"He hasn't any matches on him," she shouted. "Not a single one."

"Confound the luck!" muttered John Dolittle.

And then there was a solemn silence in the lighthouse while the Doctor above and Dab-Dab below thought gloomily of that big ship sailing onward to her wreck because they had no matches.

But suddenly out of the black stillness came a small, sweet voice singing somewhere near.

"Dab-Dab!" cried the Doctor in a whisper. "Do you hear that? A canary! There's a canary singing somewhere—probably in a cage in the lighthouse kitchen!"

In a moment he was clattering down the stairs.

"Come on," he cried. "We must find the kitchen. That canary will know where the matches are kept. Find the kitchen!"

Then the two of them went stumbling around in the darkness, feeling the walls, and presently they came upon a low door, opened it, and fell headlong down a short flight of steps that led to the lighthouse kitchen. This was a little underground room, like a cellar, cut out of the rock on which the lighthouse stood. If there was any fire or stove in it it had long since gone out, for the darkness here was as black as anywhere else. But as soon as the door had opened, the trills of the songbird grew louder.

"Tell me," called John Dolittle, in canary language, "where are the matches? Quick!"

"Oh, at last you've come," said a high, small, polite voice out of the darkness. "Would you mind putting a cover over my cage? There's a draft and I can't sleep. Nobody's been near me since midday. I don't know what can have happened to the keeper. He always covers up my cage at tea-time. But tonight I wasn't covered at all, so I went on singing. You'll find my cover up on the—"

"*Matches! Matches!* Where are the matches?" screamed Dab-Dab. "The light's out and there's a ship in danger! Where are the matches kept?"

"On the mantelpiece, next to the pepper box," said the canary. "Come over here to my cage and feel along to your left—high up—and your hand will fall right on them."

The Doctor sprang across the room, upsetting a chair on his way, and felt along the wall. His hand touched the corner of a stone shelf and the next moment Dab-Dab gave a

"The Doctor lit the candle"

deep sigh of relief, for she heard the cheerful rattle of a box of matches as the Doctor fumbled to strike a light.

"You'll find a candle on the table—there—look—behind you," said the canary, when the match light dimly lit up the kitchen.

With trembling fingers the Doctor lit the candle. Then, shielding the flame with his hand, he bounded out of the room and up the stairs.

"At last!" he muttered. "Let's hope I'm not too late!"

At the head of the kitchen steps he met the seagull coming into the lighthouse with two companions.

"Doctor," cried the gull, "we held off the ship as long as we could. But the stupid sailors, not knowing we were trying to save them, turned hoses on us and we had to give up. The ship is terribly near now."

Without a word the Doctor sped on up the winding steps of the tower. Around and around he went upward, till he was ready to drop from dizziness.

At length reaching the great glass lamp chamber at the top, he set down his candle and, striking two matches at once, he held one in each hand and lit the big wick in two places.

By this time Dab-Dab had gone outside again and was watching over the sea for the oncoming ship. And when at last the great light from the big lamp at the top of the tower suddenly flared out over the sea, there was the bow of the vessel, not more than a hundred yards from the rocky shore of the cape!

Then came a cry from the lookout, shouted orders from the captain, much blowing of whistles and ringing of bells. And just in time to save herself from a watery grave, the big ship swung her nose out to sea and sailed safely past upon her way.

· Chapter 4 ·

GULLS AND SHIPS

The morning sun peeping in at the window of the lighthouse found the Doctor still working over the keeper where he lay at the foot of the tower stairs.

"He's coming to," said Dab-Dab. "See, his eyes are beginning to blink."

"Get me some more clean water from the kitchen," said the Doctor, who was bathing a large lump on the side of the man's head.

Presently the keeper opened his eyes wide and stared up into the Doctor's face.

"Who? . . .What?" . . . he murmured stupidly. "The light! I must attend to the light! . . . I must attend to the light!" and he struggled weakly to get up.

"It's all right," said the Doctor. "The light has been lit. And it's nearly day now. Here, drink this. Then you'll feel better."

And the Doctor held some medicine to his lips that he had taken from the little black bag.

In a short while the man grew strong enough to stand on

HUGH LOFTING

"The Doctor and Dab-Dab cooked his breakfast for him"

his feet. Then with the Doctor's help he walked as far as the kitchen, where John Dolittle and Dab-Dab made him comfortable in an armchair, lit the stove, and cooked his breakfast for him.

"I'm mighty grateful to you, stranger, whoever you be," said the man. "Usually there's two of us here, me and my partner, Fred. But yesterday morning I let Fred go off with the ketch to get oysters. That's why I'm alone. I was coming down the stairs about noon, from putting new wicks in the lamp, when my foot slipped and I took a tumble to the bottom. My head fetched up against the wall and knocked the senses right out of me. How long I lay there before you found me I don't know."

"Well, all's well that ends well," said the Doctor. "Take this—you must be nearly starved." And he handed the keeper a large cup of steaming coffee.

About ten o'clock in the morning Fred, the partner, re-turned in the little sailboat from his oyster-gathering expe-dition. He was very much worried when he heard of the accident. Fred, like the other keeper, was a Londoner and a seaman. He was a pleasant fellow and both he and his partner (who was now almost entirely recovered from his injury) were very glad of the Doctor's company to break the tiresome dullness of their lonely life.

They took John Dolittle all over the lighthouse, and out-side they showed him with great pride the tiny garden of tomatoes and nasturtiums that they had planted near the foot of the tower.

They only got a holiday once a year, they told John Dolittle, when a government ship stopped near Cape Ste-phen and took them back to England for six weeks' vaca-tion, leaving two other men in their place to take care of the light while they were gone.

They asked the Doctor if he could give them any news of their beloved London. But he had to admit that he also had been away from that city for a long time. However, while they were talking Cheapside came into the lighthouse kitchen, looking for the Doctor. The city sparrow was de-lighted to find that the keepers were also cockneys. And he gave them, through the Doctor, all the latest gossip of

Wapping, Limehouse, the East India Docks, and the wharves and the shipping of London River.

The two keepers thought that the Doctor was surely crazy when he started a conversation of chirps with Cheapside. But from the answers they got to their questions, they could see there was no fake about the news of the city which the sparrow gave.

Cheapside said the faces of those two cockney seamen were the best scenery he had looked on since he had come to Africa. And after that first visit he was always flying over to the lighthouse in his spare time to see his new friends. Of course, he couldn't talk to them because neither of them knew sparrow talk—not even cockney sparrow talk. But Cheapside loved being with them, anyway.

The lighthouse keepers were sorry to have the Doctor go and they wouldn't let him leave till he promised to come and take dinner with them next Sunday.

Then, after they had loaded his canoe with a bushel of rosy tomatoes and a bouquet of nasturtiums, the Doctor, with Dab-Dab and Cheapside, paddled away for Fantippo, while the keepers waved to them from the lighthouse door.

The Doctor had not paddled very far on his return journey to the post office when the seagull who had brought the news of the light overtook him.

"Everything all right now, Doctor?" he asked as he swept in graceful circles around the canoe.

"Yes," said John Dolittle, munching a tomato. "The man got an awful crack on the head from that fall. But he will be all over it in a little while. If it hadn't been for the canary, though, who told us where the matches were—and for you, too, holding back the sailors—we would never have saved that ship."

The Doctor threw a tomato skin out of the canoe and the gull caught it neatly in the air before it touched the water.

"Well, I'm glad we were in time," said the bird.

"Tell me," asked the Doctor, "what made you come and bring me the news about the light? Gulls don't, as a rule, bother much about people or what happens to ships, do they?"

"You're mistaken, Doctor," said the gull, catching another skin with deadly accuracy. "Why, if it wasn't for the ships in the winter, we gulls would often have a hard time finding enough to eat. You see, after it gets cold fish and sea foods become sort of scarce. Sometimes we make out by going up the rivers to towns and hanging about the artificial lakes in parks where fancy waterfowl are kept. The people come to the parks and throw biscuits into the lakes for the waterfowl. But if we are around the biscuits get caught before they hit the lake—like that," and the gull snatched a third tomato skin on the wing with a lightning lunge.

"But you were speaking of ships," said the Doctor.

"Yes," the gull went on—rather indistinctly, because his mouth was full of tomato skin—"we find ships much better for winter feeding. Why, two years ago I and a cousin of mine lived the whole year round following ships for the food scraps the stewards threw out into the sea. The rougher the weather, the more food we get because then the passengers don't feel like eating and most of the grub gets thrown out."

"Ah!" said the Doctor, looking up from his paddling. "See, we are already back at the post office. And there's the pushmi-pullyu ringing the lunch bell. We're just in time. I smell liver and bacon—these tomatoes will go with it

"The gull caught the tomato skin neatly in the air"

splendidly. Won't you come in and join us?" he asked the gull. "I would like to hear more about your life with ships. You've given me an idea."

"Thank you," said the gull.

When the canoe was tied up they went into the houseboat and sat down to lunch at the kitchen table.

"Well, now," said the Doctor to the gull as soon as they were seated, "about fogs. What do you do yourself in that kind of weather—I mean, you can't see any more in the fog than the sailors can, can you?"

"No," said the gull, "we can't *see* any more, it is true. We fly up above it—way up where the air is clear. Then we can find our way as well as ever."

"I see," said the Doctor. "But the storms, what do you do in them to keep yourselves safe?"

"We seagulls never try to battle our way against a real gale. We fly with the storm—just let it carry us where it will. Then when the wind dies down we come back and finish our journey.

"We seabirds spend nearly all our lives, night and day— spring, summer, autumn, and winter—*looking at the sea*. And what is the result?" asked the gull, taking a fresh piece of toast from the rack that Dab-Dab handed him. "The result is this: we *know* the sea. Why, Doctor, if you were to shut me up in a little box with no windows in it and take me out into the middle of any ocean you liked and then opened the box and let me look at the sea—even if there wasn't a speck of land in sight—I could tell you what ocean it was and, almost to a mile, what part of it we were in. But, of course, I'd have to know what date it was."

"Marvelous!" cried the Doctor. "How do you do it?"

"From the color of it; from the little particles of things that float in it; from the kind of fishes and sea creatures swimming in it; from the way the little ripples rippled and the big waves waved; from the smell of it; from the taste, the saltness of it; and a couple of hundred other things. But, you know, in most cases—not always, but in most cases—I could tell you where we were with my eyes shut, as soon as I got out of the box, just from the wind blowing on my feathers."

"The gull took a fresh piece of toast"

"Great heavens!" the Doctor exclaimed. "You don't say!"

"When you've spent most of your life flying among the winds, using them to climb on, to swoop on, and to hover on, you get to know that there's a lot more to a wind besides its direction and its strength. How often it puffs upward or downward, how often it grows weak or grows strong, will tell you—if you know the science of winds—a whole lot."

· Chapter 5 ·

WEATHER BUREAUS

When the lunch was over the Doctor took an armchair beside the kitchen stove and lit his pipe. "I am thinking," he said to the gull, "of starting a new department in my post office. Many of the birds who have helped me in this mail business seem to be remarkably good weather prophets. And what you have just told me about your knowledge of the sea and storms has given me the idea of opening a weather bureau."

"What's that?" asked Jip, who was brushing up the table crumbs, to be put out later for the birds on the houseboat deck.

"A weather bureau," said the Doctor, "is a very important thing—especially for shipping and farmers. It is an office for telling you what kind of weather you're going to have."

"How do they do it?" asked Gub-Gub.

"They don't," said the Doctor. "At least they do sometimes. But as often as not, they're wrong. I think I can do

"The Doctor took an armchair beside the kitchen stove"

much better with my birds. They very seldom go wrong in prophesying the weather."

"Well, for what parts of the world do you want to know the weather, Doctor?" asked the gull. "If it's just for Fantippo or West Africa it will be easy as pie. All you ever get here is tornadoes. The rest of the year is just frying heat. But if you want to prophesy the weather for those countries where they have all sorts of fancy weathers, it will be a different matter. Even prophesying the weather for

England would keep you busy. Myself, I never thought that the weather itself knew what it was going to do next in England."

"The English climate's all right," put in Cheapside, his feathers ruffling up for a fight. "Don't you get turning up your long nautical nose at England, my lad. What do you call this 'ere? A climate? Well, I should call it a Turkish bath. In England we like variety in our climate. And we get it."

"I would like," said the Doctor, "to be able to prophesy weather for every part of the world. I really don't see why I shouldn't; this office, together with my branch offices, is in communication with birds going to every corner of the earth. I could improve the farming and the agriculture of the whole human race. But also, and especially, I want to have a bureau for ocean weather, to help the ships."

"Ah," said the gull, "for land weather I wouldn't be much help to you. But when it comes to the oceans, I know a bird who can tell you more about sea weather than any bureau ever knew."

"Oh," said the Doctor, "who is that?"

"We call him One Eye," said the gull. "He's an old, old albatross. Nobody knows how old. He lost an eye fighting with a fish eagle over a flounder. But he's the most marvelous weather prophet that ever lived. All seabirds have the greatest respect for his opinions. He has never been known to make a mistake."

"Indeed?" said the Doctor. "I would like very much to meet him."

"I'll get him for you," said the gull. "His home is not very far from here—out on a rock off the Angola coast. I'll go and tell him right away."

"That will be splendid," said the Doctor.

So the gull, after thanking the Doctor and Dab-Dab for a very excellent luncheon, took a couple of postcards that were going to Angola and flew off to get One Eye, the albatross.

Later in the afternoon the gull returned and with him came the great One Eye, oldest of bird weather prophets.

He agreed with the Doctor that the idea of a bird weather bureau was quite a possible thing and would lead to much better weather reports than had so far been possible. Then for a whole hour and a half he gave the Doctor a lecture on winds. Every word of this John Dolittle wrote down in a notebook.

The next thing that the Doctor did was to write to all the branch postmasters and have them arrange exactly with the different kinds of birds a time for them to start their yearly migrations—not just the second week in November, or anything like that—but an exact day and hour. Then by knowing how fast each kind of bird flies, he could calculate almost to a minute what time they should arrive at their destination. And if they were late in arriving, then he would know that bad weather had delayed them on the way or that they had put off their starting till storms died down.

The Doctor, the gull, One Eye, Dab-Dab, Cheapside, Speedy-the-Skimmer, and Too-Too the mathematician put their heads together and discussed far into the night, working out a whole lot more arrangements and particulars for running a good weather bureau. And a few weeks later a second brand-new notice board appeared on the walls of the Doctor's post office, beside the one for Outgoing and Incoming Mails.

The new notice board was marked at the top *Weather Reports,* and would read something like this:

The green herons were one day, three hours, and nine minutes late in their arrival at Cape Horn from the Sandwich Islands. Wind coming south-southeast. Blustery weather can be expected along the west coast of Chili and light gales in the Antarctic Sea.

And then the land birds, particularly those that live on berries, were very helpful to the Doctor in telling him by letter if the winter was going to be a hard one or not in their particular country. And he used to write to farmers all over the world, advising them whether they could expect a sharp frost, a wet spring, or a dry summer—which, of course, helped them in their farming tremendously.

And then the Fantippans, who so far had been very timid about going far out to sea on account of storms, now that they had a good weather bureau and knew what weather to expect, began building larger sailboats, instead of their little frail canoes. And they traded up and down the shores of West Africa, and even went as far south as the Cape of Good Hope and entered the Indian Ocean to traffic in goods with people of foreign lands.

This made the kingdom of Fantippo much richer and more important than it had been before, of course. And a large grant of money was given by the King to the foreign-mail post office, which was used by the Doctor in making the houseboat better and bigger.

And soon the No-Man's-Land weather bureau began to get known abroad. The farmers in England, who had

"John Dolittle saw him snooping around the post office"

received such good weather reports by letter from the Doctor, went up to London and told the government that their own reports were no good, that a certain John Dolittle, M.D., was writing them much better reports from someplace in Africa.

And the government got quite worked up about it. And they sent the Royal Meteorologist, an old grayhaired weatherman, down to Fantippo to see how the Doctor was doing it.

John Dolittle saw him one day, snooping around the post office, looking at the notice boards and trying to find out things. But he found out nothing. And when he got back to England he said to the government, "He hasn't any new instruments at all. The man's a fake. All he has down there is an old barge and a whole lot of messy birds flying around."

· Chapter 6 ·

TEACHING BY MAIL

The educational side of the Doctor's post office was a very important one and it grew all the time. As soon as the birds and animals realized the helpfulness of having a post office of their own, they used it more and more.

And, of course, as Speedy had foretold, they wrote most of their letters to the Doctor. Soon the poor man was swamped with mail, asking for medical advice. The Eskimo sled dogs wrote all the way from the Arctic continent to know what they should do about their hair falling out. Hair—which was all the poor creatures had to keep them warm against the polar winds—was, of course, very important to them.

And John Dolittle spent a whole Saturday and Sunday experimenting with hair tonics on Jip to find a way to cure their trouble. Jip was very patient about it, knowing that the Doctor was doing it for the good of his fellow dogs. And he did not grumble—although he did mention to Dab-Dab that he felt like a chemist's shop from all the different hair oils the Doctor had used on him. He said they ruined

HUGH LOFTING

"The Doctor experimented on Jip"

his keen nose entirely for two weeks, so he couldn't smell straight.

And besides the letters asking for medical advice, the Doctor got all sorts of requests from animals all over the world for information about food for their babies, nesting materials, and a thousand other things. In their new thirst for education the animals asked all manner of questions, some of which neither the Doctor nor anybody else could answer: What were the stars made of? Why did the tide rise and fall—and could it be stopped?

Then, in order to deal with this wide demand for information that had been brought about by his post office, John Dolittle started, for the first time in history, courses by correspondence for animals.

And he had printed forms made, called "Things a Young Rabbit Should Know," "The Care of Feet in Frosty Weather," etc., etc. These he sent out by mail in thousands.

And then, because so many letters were written him about good manners and proper behavior, he wrote *A Book of Etiquette for Animals*. It is still a very famous work, though copies of it are rare now. But when he wrote it the Doctor printed a first edition of fifty thousand copies and sent them all out by mail in one week. It was at this time, too, that he wrote and circulated another very well-known book of his called *One-Act Plays for Penguins*.

But, alas!, instead of making the number of letters he had to answer less, the Doctor found that by sending out books of information he increased a hundredfold the already enormous mail he had to attend to.

This is a letter he received from a pig in Patagonia:

Dear Doctor,

I have read your *Book of Etiquette for Animals* and liked it very much. I am shortly to be married. Would it be proper for me to ask the guests to bring turnips to my wedding, instead of flowers?

In introducing one well-bred pig to another should

you say, "Miss Virginia Ham, *meet* Mr. Frank Footer," or
"Get acquainted?"

Yours truly,
Bertha Bacon

P.S. I have always worn my engagement ring in my
nose. Is this the right place?

And the Doctor wrote back:

Dear Bertha,

In introducing one pig to another I would avoid using
the word *meet. Get acquainted* is quite all right. Remember that the object of all etiquette and manners should
be to make people comfortable—not uncomfortable.

I think turnips at a wedding are quite proper. You
might ask the guests to leave the tops on. They will then
look more like a bouquet.

Sincerely yours,
John Dolittle

PART THREE

· Chapter 1 ·

THE ANIMALS' MAGAZINE

The next thing I must tell you about is the prize-story competition: The Puddleby fireside circle, where the Doctor had amused his pets with so many interesting tales, had become quite a famous institution. Too-Too had gossiped about it; Gub-Gub, Jip, and the white mouse had boasted of it. (You see, they were always proud that they could say they were part of the great man's regular household.) And before long, through this new post office of their own, creatures all over the world were speaking of it and discussing it by letter. Next thing, the Doctor began to receive requests for stories by mail. He had become equally famous as an animal doctor, an animal educator, and an animal author.

From the far north letters came in by the dozen from polar bears and walruses and foxes asking that he send them some light entertaining reading as well as his medical pamphlets and books of etiquette. The winter nights (weeks and weeks long up there) grew frightfully monotonous, they said, after their own supply of stories had run out—because you couldn't possibly sleep *all* the time and something had to be done for amusement on the lonely ice floes and in the dens and lairs beneath the blizzard-swept snow. For some time the Doctor was kept so busy with more serious things that he was unable to attend to it. But he kept it in mind until he should be able to think out the best way of dealing with the problem.

Now his pets, after the post-office work got sort of settled and regular, often found it somewhat hard to amuse themselves in the evenings. One night they were all sitting around on the veranda of the houseboat wondering what game they could play when Jip suddenly said, "I know what we can do—let's get the Doctor to tell us a story."

"Oh, you've heard all my stories," said the Doctor. "Why don't you play Hunt-the-Slipper?"

"The houseboat isn't big enough," said Dab-Dab. "Last time we played it Gub-Gub got stuck by the pushmi-pull-yu's horns. You've got plenty of stories. Tell us one, Doctor —just a short one."

"Well, but what shall I tell you a story about?" asked John Dolittle.

"About a turnip field," said Gub-Gub.

"No, that won't do," said Jip. "Doctor, why don't you do what you did sometimes by the fire in Puddleby—turn your pockets out upon the table till you come to something that reminds you of a story—you remember?"

"All right," said the Doctor. "But—"

And then an idea came to him.

"Look here," he said, "You know I've been asked for stories by mail. The creatures around the north pole want some light reading for the long winter nights. I'm going to start an animals' magazine for them. I'm calling it *The*

Arctic Monthly. It will be sent by mail and distributed by the Nova Zembla branch office. So far, so good. But the great problem is how to get sufficient stories and pictures and articles and things to fill a monthly magazine—no easy matter. Now listen, if I tell you animals a story tonight, you'll have to do something to help me with my new magazine. Every night when you want to amuse yourselves we'll take it in turns to tell a story. That will give us seven stories right away. There will be only one story printed each month—the rest of the magazine will be news of the day, a medical advice column, a babies' and mothers' page, and odds and ends. Then we'll have a prize-story competition. The readers shall judge which is the best; and when they write to us here and tell us, we'll give the prize to the winner. What do you say?"

"What a splendid idea!" cried Gub-Gub. "I'll tell my story tomorrow night. I know a good one. Now go ahead, Doctor."

Then John Dolittle started turning his trouser pockets out onto the table to try and find something that reminded him of a story. It was certainly a wonderful collection of objects that he brought forth. There were pieces of string and pieces of wire, stub ends of pencils, pocketknives with the blades broken, coat buttons, boot buttons, a magnifying glass, a compass, and a corkscrew.

"There doesn't seem to be anything very hopeful there," said the Doctor.

"Try in your waistcoat pockets," said Too-Too. "They were always the most interesting. You haven't turned them out since you left Puddleby. There must be lots in them."

So the Doctor turned out his waistcoat pockets. These

HUGH LOFTING

"It was certainly a wonderful collection of objects"

brought forth two watches (one that went and one that didn't), a measuring tape, a piece of cobbler's wax, a penny with a hole through it, and a clinical thermometer.

"What's that?" asked Gub-Gub, pointing to the thermometer.

"That's for taking people's temperature with," said the Doctor. "Oh, that reminds me—"

"Of a story?" cried Too-Too.

"I knew it would," said Jip. "A thing like that must have a story to it. What's the name of the story, Doctor?"

"Well," said the Doctor, settling himself back in his chair, "I think I'll call this story 'The Invalids' Strike.'"

"What's a strike?" asked Gub-Gub.

"And what on earth is an invalid?" cried the pushmi-pullyu.

"A strike," said the Doctor, "is when people stop doing their own particular work in order to get somebody else to give them what they want. And an invalid . . . well, an invalid is a person who is always—er, more or less—ill."

"But what kind of work is invalids' work?" asked the white mouse.

"Their work is—er—staying ill," said the Doctor. "Stop asking questions or I'll never get this story started."

"Wait a minute," said Gub-Gub. "My foot's gone to sleep."

"Oh, bother your feet!" cried Dab-Dab. "Let the Doctor get on with his story."

"Is it a good story?" asked Gub-Gub.

"Well," said the Doctor, "I'll tell it, and then you can decide for yourself. Stop fidgeting now, and let me begin. It's getting late."

· Chapter 2 ·

THE DOCTOR'S STORY

As soon as the Doctor had lit his pipe and got it going well he began:

"Many years ago, at the time I bought this thermometer, I was a very young doctor, full of hope, just starting out in business. I fancied myself a very good doctor, but I found that the rest of the world did not seem to think so. And for many months after I began I did not get a single patient. I had no one to try my new thermometer on. I tried it on myself quite often. But I was always so frightfully healthy I never had any temperature anyway. I tried to catch a cold. I didn't really want a cold, you understand, but I did want to make sure that my new thermometer worked. But I couldn't even catch a cold. I was very sad—healthy but sad.

"Well, about this time I met another young doctor who was in the same fix as myself—having no patients. Said he to me, 'I'll tell you what we'll do, let's start a sanitarium.'"

"What's a sanitarium?" asked Gub-Gub.

"A sanitarium," said the Doctor, "is a sort of mixture

between a hospital and a hotel—where people stay who are invalids. Well, I agreed to this idea. Then I and my young friend—his name was Phipps, Dr. Cornelius Q. Phipps—took a beautiful place way off in the country, and we furnished it with wheelchairs and hot-water bottles and ear trumpets and the things that invalids like. And very soon patients came to us in hundreds and our sanitarium was quite full up and my new thermometer was kept very busy. Of course, we made a lot of money because all these people paid us well. And Phipps was very happy.

"But I was not so happy. I had noticed a peculiar thing: none of the invalids ever seemed to get well and go away. And finally I spoke of this to Phipps.

"'My dear Dolittle,' he answered. *'Go away?* Of course not! We don't want them to go away. We want them to stay here, so they'll keep on paying us.'

"'Phipps,' I said, 'I don't think that's honest. I became a doctor to cure people—not to pamper them.'

"Well, on this point we fell out and quarreled. I got very angry and told him I would not be his partner any longer —that I would pack up and go the following day. As I left his room, still very angry, I passed one of the invalids in his wheelchair. It was Sir Timothy Quisby, our most important and expensive patient. He asked me, as I passed, to take his temperature, as he thought he had a new fever. Now, I had never been able to find anything wrong with Sir Timothy and had decided that being an invalid was a sort of hobby with him. So still very angry, instead of taking his temperature, I said quite rudely, 'Oh, go to the dickens!'

"Sir Timothy was furious. And, calling for Dr. Phipps, he

"It was Sir Timothy Quisby, our most expensive patient"

demanded that I apologize. I said I wouldn't. Then Sir Timothy told Phipps that if I didn't he would start an invalids' strike. Phipps got terribly worried and implored me to apologize to this very special patient. I still refused.

"Then a peculiar thing happened. Sir Timothy, who had always so far seemed too weak to walk, got right out of his wheelchair and, waving his ear trumpet wildly, ran around all over the sanitarium, making speeches to the other invalids, saying how shamefully he had been treated, and calling on them to strike for their rights.

"And they did strike—and no mistake. That night at dinner they refused to take their medicine—either before or after meals. Dr. Phipps argued with them, prayed them, implored them to behave like proper invalids, and carry out their doctors' orders. But they wouldn't listen to him. They ate all the things they had been forbidden to eat, and after dinner those who had been ordered to go for a walk stayed at home, and those who had been ordered to stay quiet went outside and ran up and down the street. They finished the evening by having a pillow fight with their hot-water bottles, when they should have been in bed. The next morning they all packed their own trunks and left. And that was the end of *our* sanitarium.

"But the most peculiar thing of all was this: I found out afterward that every single one of those patients had gotten well! Getting out of their wheelchairs and going on strike had done them so much good they stopped being invalids altogether. As a sanitarium doctor, I suppose I was not a success—still, I don't know. Certainly I cured a great many more patients by going *out* of the sanitarium business than Phipps ever did by going into it."

· Chapter 3 ·

GUB-GUB'S STORY

The next night, when they were again seated around the veranda after supper, the Doctor asked, "Now, who's going to tell us a story tonight? Didn't Gub-Gub say he had one for us?"

"Oh, don't let him tell one, Doctor," said Jip. "It's sure to be stupid."

"He isn't old enough to tell a good story," said Dab-Dab. "He hasn't had any experience."

"His only interest in life is food, anyway," said Too-Too. "Let someone else tell a story."

"No, now wait a minute," cried the Doctor. "Don't all be jumping on him this way. We were all young once. Let him tell his story. He may win the prize. Who knows? Come along, Gub-Gub. Tell us your story. What's the name of it?"

Gub-Gub fidgeted his feet, blushed up to the ears, and finally said, "This is a kind of a crazy story. But it's a good one. It's—er—er—a piggish fairy tale. It's called 'The Magic Cucumber.' "

"Gosh!" growled Jip.

"More food!" murmured Too-Too. "What did I tell you?"

"Tee-hee-hee!" tittered the white mouse.

"Go on, Gub-Gub," said the Doctor. "Don't take any notice of them. I'm listening."

"Once upon a time," Gub-Gub began, "a small pig went out into the forest with his father to dig for truffles. The father pig was a very clever truffle digger, and just by smelling the ground he could tell with great sureness the places where truffles were to be found. Well, this day they came upon a place beneath some big oak trees and they started digging. Presently, after the father pig had dug up an enormous truffle and they were both eating it, they heard, to their great astonishment, the sound of voices coming from the hole out of which they had dug the truffle.

"The father pig hurried away with his child because he did not like magic. But that night the baby pig, when his mother and father were fast asleep, crept out of his sty and went off into the woods. He wanted to find out the mystery of those voices coming from under the ground.

"So, reaching the hole where his father had dug up the truffle, he set to work digging for himself. He had not dug very long when the earth caved right in underneath him, and he felt himself falling and falling and falling. At last he came to a stop, upside down in the middle of a dining table. The table was all set for dinner—and he had fallen into the soup. He looked about him and saw seated around the table many tiny little men, none of them more than half as big as himself and all a dark green in color.

" 'Where am I?' asked the baby pig.

" 'You're in the soup,' said the little men.

"The baby pig was at first terribly frightened. But when

"He had fallen into the soup"

he saw how small were the men around him his fear left him. And before he got out of the soup tureen on the table he drank up all the soup.

"He then asked the little men who they might be. And they said, 'We are the cook goblins. We live under the ground and we spend half our time inventing new things to eat and the other half in eating them. The noise you heard coming out of the hole was us singing our food hymns. We always sing food hymns whenever we are preparing particularly fine dishes.'

" 'Good!' said the pig. 'I've come to the right place. Let us go on with the dinner.'

"But just as they were about to begin on the fish (the soup was already gone, you see), there was a great noise outside the dining hall and in rushed another lot of little men, a bright red in color. These were the toadstool sprites, ancient enemies of the cook goblins. A tremendous fight began, one side using toothpicks for spears and the other using nutcrackers for clubs. The pig took the side of his friends the cook goblins, and, being as big as any two of the enemy put together, he soon had the toadstool sprites running for their lives.

"When the fight was over and the dining hall cleared, the cook goblins were very grateful to the baby pig for his valuable assistance. They called him a conquering hero and, crowning him with a wreath of parsley, they invited him to the seat of honor at the dining table and went on with the meal.

"Never had the baby pig enjoyed a meal so much in all his life as he did that one. He found that the cook goblins, as well as inventing new and marvelously tasty dishes, had also thought out a lot of new things in the way of table furnishings. For instance, they served pincushions with the fish. These were to stick your fishbones in, instead of leaving them to clutter up your plate. Pudding fans were another of their novelties—fans for cooling off your pudding with, instead of blowing on it. Then they had cocoa-skin clotheslines—little toy clotheslines to hang the skin off your cocoa on, neatly. (You know what a nasty mess it makes draped over the rim of your cup.) And when the fruit came on, tennis racquets were handed around also. And if anyone at the other end of the table asked you for an apple, instead of going to all the work of handing down a heavy bowl of fruit, you just took an apple and served it at him like a tennis ball, and he would catch it at the other end of the table on the point of a fork.

"These things added a good deal of jolliness to the meal, and some of them were very clever inventions. Why, they even had a speaking tube for things you are not allowed to mention at the table."

"A speaking tube!" the white mouse interrupted. "How was it used? I don't understand."

"Well," said Gub-Gub, "you know how people are always telling you 'You mustn't speak about those things at the table!' Well, the cook goblins had a speaking tube in the wall that led, at the other end, to the open air outside. And whenever you wanted to talk about any of the things forbidden at the table, you left the table and went and said it into the speaking tube; then you came back to your seat. It was a very great invention . . . Well, as I was saying, the baby pig enjoyed himself tremendously. And when the meal was over he said he must be going back because he wanted to get into the sty before his mother and father should be awake.

"The cook goblins were sorry to see him go. And as a farewell present in return for the help he had given them against their enemies, they gave him the magic cucumber. Now, this cucumber, if you cut off even the smallest part of it and planted it, would grow immediately into a whole field of any fruit or vegetable you wished. All you had to do was to say the name of the vegetable you wanted. The baby pig thanked the cook goblins, kissed them all good-bye, and went home.

"He found his mother and father still asleep when he got back. So after carefully hiding his magic cucumber under the floor of the cow barn, he crept into the sty and went fast asleep.

"Now, it happened that a few days later a neighboring king made war upon the king that owned the country where the pig family lived. Things went very badly for the pigs' king, and, seeing that the enemy were close at hand, he gave orders that all cattle and farm animals and people should be brought inside the castle walls. The pig family was also driven into the castle grounds. But before he left, the baby pig went and bit off a piece of his magic cucumber and took it along with him.

"Soon after, the enemy's army closed about the castle and tried to storm it. Then for many weeks they remained there, knowing that sooner or later the king and the people in the castle would run short of food and have to give in.

"Now, it happened that the queen had noticed the baby pig within the castle grounds and, being a princess of Irish blood, she took a great fancy to him and had a piece of green ribbon tied about his neck and made a regular pet of him, much to the disgust of her husband, the king.

"Well, the fourth week after the enemy came, the food in the castle was all gone and the king gave orders that the pigs must be eaten. The queen raised a great outcry and begged that her pet should be spared. But the king was very firm.

" 'My soldiers are starving,' said he. 'Your pet, madam, must be turned into sausages.'

"Then the baby pig saw that the time to use the goblins'

HUGH LOFTING

"She made a regular pet of him"

magic gift had come. And, rushing out into the castle garden, he dug a hole and planted his piece of cucumber right
in the middle of the king's best rosebed.

" 'Parsnips!' he grunted, as he filled in the hole. 'May they
blossom acres wide!'

"And, sure enough, he had hardly said the words before
all over the king's garden parsnips began springing up
thick and fast. Even the gravel walks were covered with
them.

"Then the king and his army had plenty of food and, growing strong on the nutritious parsnips, they sallied forth from the castle, smote the enemy, hip and thigh, and put them to flight.

"And the queen was allowed to keep her pet pig, which rejoiced her kind heart greatly—she being of Irish blood royal. And he became a great hero at the court and was given a sty studded with jewels in the center of the castle garden—on the very spot where he had planted the magic cucumber. And they all lived happily ever after. And that is the end of the piggish fairy tale."

· Chapter 4 ·

DAB-DAB'S STORY

The animals now began to look forward to the evening story-telling. For the next night they arranged that it would be Dab-Dab's turn to tell a tale.

After they were all seated on the veranda the house-keeper preened her feathers and in a very dignified voice began:

"On the outskirts of Puddleby-on-the-Marsh there lives a farmer who swears to this day that his cat can understand every word he says. It isn't true, but both the farmer and his wife think it is. And I am now going to tell you how they came to get that idea.

"Once when the Doctor was away in Scotland, looking for fossils, he left me behind to take charge of the house. The old horse in the stable complained to me one night that the rats were eating up all his corn. While I was walking around the stable, trying to think out what I should do about it I spied an enormous white Persian cat stalking about the premises. Now, I myself have no love for cats. For one thing, they eat ducklings, and for another, they always seem to me sort of sneaky things. So I ordered this one to get off the Doctor's property. To my surprise, she behaved very politely—said she didn't know she was trespassing and turned to leave. Then I felt sort of guilty, knowing the Doctor liked to be hospitable to every kind of animal, and, after all, the cat wasn't doing any harm there. So I overtook her and told her that if she didn't kill anything on the place she could come and go as she pleased.

"Well, we got chatting, the way people do, and I found out that the cat lived at a farmer's house about a quarter of a mile down the Oxenthorpe Road. Then I walked part of the way home with her, still chatting, and I found that she was a very agreeable individual. I told her about the rats in the stable and the difficulty I had in making them behave, because the Doctor wouldn't allow anyone to kill them. And she said, if I wished, she'd sleep in the stable a few nights and the rats would probably leave as soon as they smelled her around.

"This she did, and the results were excellent. The rats departed in a body and the old horse's corn bin was left undisturbed. Then she disappeared and for several nights I saw nothing of her. So one evening I thought it would be only decent of me to call at her farm down the Oxenthorpe Road, to thank her.

"I went to her farm and found her in the farmyard. I thanked her for what she had done and asked her why she hadn't been around to my place of late.

" 'I've just had kittens,' she said. 'Six—and I haven't been able to leave them a moment. They are in the farmer's parlor now. Come in and I'll show them to you.'

"So in we went. And on the parlor floor, in a round basket, there were six of the prettiest kittens you ever saw.

While we were looking at them we heard the farmer and his wife coming downstairs. So, thinking they might not like to have a duck in the parlor (some folks are so snobbish and persnickety, you know—not like the Doctor), I hid myself behind a closet door just as the farmer and his wife came into the room.

"They leaned over the basket of kittens, stroked the white cat, and started talking. Now, the cat didn't understand what they said, of course. But I, being around the Doctor so much and discussing with him the differences between duck grammar and people's grammar, understood every word they uttered.

"And this is what I heard the farmer say to his wife: 'We'll keep the black and white kitten, Liza. I'll drown the other five tomorrow morning. Won't never do to have all them cats running around the place.' His grammar was atrocious.

"As soon as they had gone I came out of the closet and I said to the white cat, 'I shall expect you to bring up these kittens to leave ducklings alone. Now listen: Tonight, after the farmer and his wife are in bed, take all your kittens *except the black and white one,* and hide them in the attic. The farmer means to drown them and is going to keep only one.'

"The cat did as I bade her. And next morning, when the farmer came to take the kittens away, he found only the black and white one—the one he meant to keep. He could not understand it. Some weeks later, however, when the farmer's wife was spring-cleaning, she came upon the others in the attic, where the mother cat had hidden them and nursed them secretly. But they were now grown big

" 'We'll keep the black and white one, Liza' "

enough to escape through the window, and they went off to find new homes for themselves.

"And that is why to this day that farmer and his wife swear their cat can understand English—because, they say, she must have heard them when they were talking over the basket. And whenever she's in the room and they are gossiping about the neighbors, they always speak in whispers, lest she overhear. But between you and me, she doesn't really understand a single word they say."

· Chapter 5 ·

THE WHITE MOUSE'S STORY

Who's turn is it to give us a story now?"
asked the Doctor, when the supper things were cleared
away the following evening.

"I think the white mouse ought to tell us one," said Jip.

"Very well," said the white mouse. "I will tell you one
about the days of my youth. The Doctor knows this story,
but the rest of you have never heard it."

And smoothing back his white whiskers and curling his
pink tail snugly about his small, sleek body, he blinked his
eyes twice and began:

"When I was born I was one of seven twins. But all my
brothers and sisters were ordinary mouse color and I
alone out of the whole family was white. My color worried
my mother and father a great deal. They said I was so
conspicuous and would certainly, as soon as I left the nest,
get caught by the first owl or cat that came along.

"We were city folk, my family were—and proud of it. We
lived under the floor of a miller's shop. Across the street
from our place was a butcher's shop, and next door to us

142

was a dyer's—where they dyed cloth different colors before it went to the tailor's to be made into suits.

"Now, when we children grew up big enough to go off for ourselves, our parents gave us all sorts of careful instructions about escaping cats and ferrets and weasels and dogs. But over poor me they shook their heads. They really felt that there was not much hope of my leading a peaceful life, with white fur that could be seen a mile off.

"Well, they were quite right. My color got me into trouble the first week that I set out to seek my fortune—but not in the way they thought it would. The son of the miller who owned the shop where we lived found me one morning in a bin of oats.

" 'Aha!' he cried. 'A white mouse! The very thing I've been wanting!'

"And he caught me in a fishing net and put me in a cage, to keep as a pet.

"I was very sad at first. But after a while I got sort of used to the life. The boy—he was only eight years old— treated me kindly and fed me regularly each day. I grew almost fond of the funny, snub-nosed lad and became so tame that he would let me out of my cage sometimes, and I would run up and down his sleeve. But I never got a chance to escape.

"After some months I began to grow weary of the silly life I was leading. And then, too, the wild mice were so mean to me. They used to come around at night and point at me through the wire of my cage, saying, 'Look at the tame white mouse! Tee-hee-hee! A plaything for children! Good little mousie! Come and have 'ims facey washed!' The stupid little idiots!

"Well, finally I set to work and thought out a clever plan

of escape. I gnawed a hole through the wooden floor of my cage and kept it covered with straw, so the boy couldn't see it. And one night when I heard him safely snoring—he always kept my cage at the head of his bed—I slipped out of the hole and got away.

"I had many adventures with cats. It was wintertime and the snow lay thick upon the ground. I started off to explore the world, rejoicing in my liberty. Going around to the back of the house, I passed from the miller's yard into the dyer's yard, next door. In the yard was a dyeing shed and I noticed two owls sitting on the top of it in the moonlight.

"Entering the shed, I met a rat, very old and very thin. Said he to me, 'I am the oldest rat in the town and I know a great deal. But, tell me, why do you come here into the dyeing shed?'

" 'I was looking for food,' I said.

"The old rat laughed a cracked and quavering laugh, with no joy in it at all.

" 'There's no food here,' he said, 'only dyes of different colors.' And he pointed to the big dye vats, all in a row, that towered in the half darkness above our heads.

" 'Any food there was here I've eaten,' he went on sadly, 'and I dare not go out for more because the owls are waiting on the roof. They'd see my dark body against the snow and I'd stand no chance of escape. I am nearly starved.' And he swayed weakly on his old feet. 'But now you've come, it's different. Some good fairy must have sent you to me. I've been sitting here for days and nights on end, hoping a white mouse might come along. With your white fur, you understand, the owls can't see you so well against the snow. That's what's called *protective coloration*. I know all about natural history—I'm very old, you see. That is why

"The old rat laughed a quavering laugh"

you managed to get in here without being caught. Go out now, for pity's sake, and bring me the first food of any kind that you can find. The owls by night and the cats by day have kept me shut in here since the snow came, without a bite to eat. You are only just in time to save my life.'

"So off I went across the moonlit snow and the blinking owls on the roof of the dyeing shed never spotted me. Against the whiteness I was nearly invisible. I felt quite proud. At last my white fur was coming in handy.

"I found a garbage can and, picking out some bacon rinds, I carried them back to the starving rat. The old fellow was ever so grateful. He ate and ate—my whiskers, how he ate! Finally he said, 'Ah! Now I feel better.'

" 'You know,' said I, 'I have only just escaped from captivity. I was kept as a pet by a boy. So far, being white has only been a great inconvenience to me. The cats could see me so well life wasn't worth living.'

" 'Well, now, I'll tell you what we'll do,' said he, 'you come and live in this dyeing shed with me. It isn't a bad place—quite warm and snug under the floors, and the foundations are simply riddled with holes and corridors and hiding places. And while the snow is here you can go out and get the food for both of us—because you can't be seen so well against the snow. And when the winter is over and the earth is black again *I* will do the food hunting outside and *you* can do the staying at home. You see, this is a good place to live in in another way—there is nothing for rats and mice to destroy here, so people don't bother about you. Other places—like houses and food shops and mills— folks are always setting traps and sending ferrets after you. But no one minds rats living in a dyeing shed, see? Foolish young rats and mice go and live where there's lots of food. But not for me! I'm a wise one, I am.'

"Well, we agreed upon this arrangement and for a whole year I lived at the dyer's with the old wise rat. And we lived high—no mistake! Not a soul ever bothered us. In the winter days I did the foraging and when summer came my old partner, who knew where to get the choicest foods in town, kept our larder stocked with the daintiest delicacies. Ah, many's the jolly meal I've had under the floor of the dye shed with that old veteran, chuckling in whispers as

we heard the dyers overhead mixing the dyes in the great
big vats and talking over the news of the town!

"But none of us are ever content for long, you know—
foolish creatures that we are. And by the time the second
summer was coming I was longing to be a free mouse, to
roam the world and all that sort of thing. And then, too, I
wanted to get married. Maybe spring was getting into my
blood.

"So one night I said to the old rat, 'Rat,' I said, 'I'm in
love. All winter, every night I went out to gather fodder,
I've been keeping company with a lady mouse—well-bred
she is, with elegant manners. I've a mind to settle down
and have a family of my own. Now, here comes the summer again and I've got to stay shut up in this miserable
shed on account of my beastly color.'

"The old rat gazed at me thoughtfully a moment and I
knew that he was going to say something particularly wise.

" 'Young man,' says he at last, 'if you've a mind to go I
reckon I can't stop you—foolish young madcap though I
think you. And how I'll ever shift for myself after you've
gone, goodness only knows. But, seeing you have been so
useful to me this past year and more, I'll help you.'

"So saying, he takes me upstairs to where the dye vats
stood. It was twilight and the men were gone. But we could
see the dim shapes of the big vats towering above our
heads. Then he takes a string that lay upon the floor and,
scaling up the middle vat, he lets the string down inside.

" 'What's that for?' I asked.

" 'That's for you to climb out by, after you've taken a
bath. For you to go abroad in summer with a coat like
yours would mean certain death. So I'm going to dye you
black.'

HUGH LOFTING

"Upstairs where the dye vats stood"

" 'Jumping Cheese!' I cried. *Dye me black!*'

" 'Just that,' says he. 'It's quite simple. Scale up that middle vat now—onto the edge—and dive right in. Don't be afraid. There's a string there for you to climb out by.'

"Well, I was always adventurous by nature. And, plucking up my courage, I scrambled up the vat, onto the edge of it. It was awful dark and I could just see the dye, glimmering murky and dim, far down inside.

" 'Go ahead,' said the old rat. 'Don't be afraid—and be sure you dip your head and all under.'

"Well, it took an awful lot of nerve to take that plunge. And if I hadn't been in love I don't suppose I'd ever have done it. But I did—I dove right down into the dye.

"I thought I'd never come up again, and even when I did I nearly drowned before I found the string in the dark and scrambled, gasping for breath, out of the vat.

" 'Fine!' says the old rat. 'Now run around the shed a few times, so you won't take a chill. And then go to bed and cover up. In the morning when it's light you'll find yourself very different.'

"Well—tears come to my eyes when I think of it—the next day, when I woke up, expecting to find myself a smart, decent black, I found instead that I had dyed myself a bright and gaudy *blue*! That stupid old rat had made a mistake in the vats!"

The white mouse paused a moment in his story, as though overcome with emotion. Presently he went on, "Never have I been so furious with anyone in my life as I was with that old rat.

" 'Look! *Look* what you've done to me now!' I cried. 'It isn't even a navy-blue. You've made me just hideous!'

" 'I can't understand it,' he murmured. 'The middle vat *used* to be the black one, I know. They must have changed them. The blue one was always the one on the left.'

" 'You're a stupid old duffer!' I said. And I left the dye shed in great anger and never went back to it again.

"Well, if I had been conspicuous before, now I was a hundred times more so. Against the black earth or the green grass or the white snow or brown floors, my loud, sky-blue coat could be seen as plain as a pikestaff. The minute I got outside the shed a cat jumped for me. I gave her the slip and got out into the street. There some wretched children spotted me and, calling to their friends that they had seen a blue mouse, they hunted me along the gutter. At the corner of the street two dogs were fighting. They stopped their fight and joined the chase after me. And very soon I had the whole blessed town at my heels. It was awful. I didn't get any peace till after night had fallen, and by that time I was so exhausted with running I was ready to drop.

"About midnight I met the lady mouse with whom I was in love, beneath a lamppost. And, would you believe it? She wouldn't speak to me! Cut me dead, she did.

" 'It was for your sake I got myself into this beastly mess,' I said, as she stalked by me with her nose in the air. 'You're an ungrateful woman, that's what you are.'

" 'Oh, la, la, la!' said she, smirking. 'You wouldn't expect any self-respecting person to keep company with a *blue* mouse, would you?'

"Later, when I was trying to find a place to sleep, all the mice I met, wherever there was any light at all, made fun of me and pointed at me and jeered. I was nearly in tears. Then I went down to the river, hoping I might wash the dye off and so get white again. That, at least, would be better than the way I was now. But I washed and I swam and I rinsed, all to no purpose. Water made no impression on me.

"So there I sat, shivering on the riverbank, in the depths of despair. And presently I saw the sky in the east growing pale and I knew that morning was coming. Daylight! That for me meant more hunting and running and jeering, as soon as the sun should show my ridiculous color.

"And then I came to a very sad decision—probably the saddest decision that a free mouse ever made. Rather than be hunted and jeered at any more I decided that I would sooner be back in a cage, a pet mouse! Yes, there at least I was well treated and well fed by the snub-nosed miller lad. I would go back and be a captive mouse. Was I not spurned by my ladylove and jeered at by my friends? Very well then, I would turn my back upon the world and go into captivity. And then my lady love would be sorry—too late!

"So, picking myself up wearily, I started off for the miller's shop. On the threshold I paused a moment. It was a terrible step I was about to take. I gazed miserably down the street, thinking upon the hardness of life and the sadness of love, and there, coming toward me, with a bandage around his tail, was my own brother!

"As he took a seat beside me on the doorstep I burst into tears and told him all that had happened to me since we left our parents' home.

" 'I am terribly sorry for your bad luck,' said he when I had ended. 'But I'm glad I caught you before you went back into captivity. Because I think I can guide you to a way out of your troubles.'

" 'What way is there?' I said. 'For me, life is over!'

" 'Go and see the Doctor,' said my brother.

" 'What doctor?' I asked.

" 'There *is* only one Doctor,' he answered. 'You don't mean to say you've never *heard* of him!'

"And then he told me all about Doctor Dolittle. This was around the time when the Doctor first began to be famous among the animals. But I, living alone with the old rat at the dyer's shed, had not heard the news.

" 'I've just come from the Doctor's office,' said my

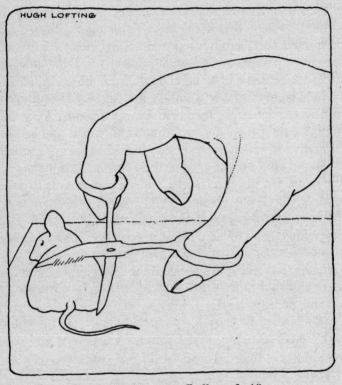

HUGH LOFTING

" 'The Doctor cut off all my fur' "

brother. 'I got my tail caught in a trap and he bandaged it up for me. He's a marvelous man—kind and honest. And he talks animals' language. Go to him and I'm sure he'll know some way to clean blue dye off a mouse. He knows everything.'

"So that is how I first came to John Dolittle's house in Puddleby. The Doctor, when I told my troubles to him, took a very small pair of scissors and cut off all my fur, so I was as bald and as pink as a pig. Then he rubbed me with some special hair restorer for mice—a patent invention of his own. And very soon I grew a brand-new coat of fur as white as snow!

"And then, hearing what difficulty I had had keeping away from cats, the Doctor gave me a home in his own house—in his own piano, in fact. And no mouse could wish for more than that. He even offered to send for the lady I was in love with, who would, no doubt, think differently about me, now that I was white again.

"But I said, 'No, Doctor. Let her be. I'm through with women for good.'"

· Chapter 6 ·
JIP'S STORY

The next night Jip was called upon for a story. And after thinking a moment he said, "All right, I'll tell you the story of 'The Beggar's Dog.'" And the animals all settled down to listen attentively because Jip had often told them stories before and they liked his way of telling them.

"Some time ago," Jip began, "I knew a dog who was a beggar's dog. We met by chance one day, when a butcher's cart had an accident and got upset. The butcher's boy who was driving the cart was a stupid boy whom all the dogs of that town heartily disliked. So when his cart hit a lamppost and overturned, spilling mutton chops and joints all over the street, we dogs were quickly on the scene and ran off with all his meat before he had time to pick himself up out of the gutter.

"It was on this occasion, as I said, that I fell in with the beggar's dog. I found him bolting down the street beside me, with a choice steak flapping merrily around his ears. Myself, I had pinched a string of sausages and the beastly things kept getting tangled up in my legs—till he came to my rescue and showed me how to coil them up neatly, so I could run with them without getting tripped.

"After that the beggar's dog and I became great friends. I found that his master had only one leg and was very, very old.

" 'He's most frightfully poor,' said my friend. 'And he's too old to work, you see—even if he had two legs to get around on. And now he has taken to pavement art. You know what that is—you draw pictures on the pavement in colored chalks and you write under them *All my own work*. And then you sit by the side of them, with your cap in your hand, waiting for people to give you pennies.'

" 'Oh, yes,' I said, 'I know. I've seen pavement artists before.'

" 'Well,' said my friend, 'my beggar doesn't get any pennies. And I know the reason why: his pictures aren't good enough—not even for pavement art. Myself, I don't pretend to know much about drawing. But his pictures are just awful—*awful*. One kind old lady the other day stopped before our stand—wanting to encourage him, you know—and, pointing to one picture, she said, *"Oh, what a lovely tree!"* The picture was meant to be a lighthouse in the middle of the ocean, with a storm raging around it. That's the kind of an artist my man is. I don't know what to do about him.'

" 'Well, look here,' I said, 'I have an idea. Since your man can't work for himself, suppose you and I go into the bone-hiring business.'

" 'What on earth is that?' he asked.

" 'Well,' I said, 'people hire out bicycles and pianos for rent, don't they? So, why can't you and I rent out bones for dogs to chew? They won't be able to pay us in money, of

" 'His pictures are just awful' "

course, so we'll get them to bring us things, instead. Then the beggar can sell the things and get money.'

" 'That's a good notion,' said he. 'Let's start tomorrow.' "

"So the following day we found an empty lot, where people used to dump rubbish, and dug an enormous hole, which was to be our bone shop. Then we went around to the back doors of all the richest people's houses early in the morning and picked out the best bones from the garbage cans. We even snatched a few from other dogs who were tied to kennels and couldn't run after us—rather a dirty trick, but we were working in a good cause and were not particular.

"Then we took all these bones and put them in the hole we had dug. By night we kept them covered up with earth because we didn't want them stolen—and, besides, some dogs prefer their bones buried a few days before they chew them. It gets them seasoned-like. And then by day we stood over our wares, calling out to all the dogs that passed by, 'Bones for hire! Beef bones, ham bones, mutton bones, chicken bones! All juicy! Step up, gentlemen, and take your choice! BONES for hire!'

"Well, right from the start we did a roaring trade. All the dogs for miles around heard of us and came to hire bones. And we would charge them according to the length of time they wanted to hire them. For instance, you could rent a good ham bone for one day for a candlestick or a hair-brush, for three days for a violin or an umbrella. And if you wanted your bone for a whole week, you had to bring us a suit of clothes in payment.

"Well, for a while our plan worked splendidly. The beggar sold the things that we got in payment from the dogs and he had money to live on.

"But we never thought where the dogs might be getting all these things they brought us. The truth is, we didn't bother very much, I'm afraid. Anyway, at the end of our first week of brisk trade we noticed a great many people going through the streets as though they were looking for something. And presently these people, seeing our shop in the empty lot, gathered around us, talking to one another.

"A retriever came up with a gold watch and chain"

And while they were talking a retriever came up to me with a gold watch and chain in his mouth, which he wanted to exchange for a ham bone.

"Well, you should have seen the excitement among the people then! The owner of the watch and chain was there and he raised a terrible row. And then it came out that these dogs had been taking things from their masters' homes to hire bones with. The people were dreadfully annoyed. They closed up our bone shop and put us out of business. But they never discovered that the money we had made had gone to the beggar.

"Of course, we hadn't made enough to keep him in comfort for long and very soon he had to become a pavement artist again and was as badly off as he had ever been—and the pictures he drew were worse, if anything, than before.

"Now it happened one day, when I was wandering around in the country outside the town, that I met a most conceited spaniel. He passed me with his nose turned up in the air in such a cheeky manner that I said to him, I said, 'What makes you so stuck up?'

" 'My master has been ordered to paint the portrait of a prince,' he said, putting on no end of elegance.

" 'Who is your master?' I said. 'Anybody would think you were going to paint the portrait yourself.'

" 'My master is a very famous artist,' said he.

" 'What's his name?' I asked.

" 'George Morland,' said the spaniel.

" 'George Morland!' I cried. 'Is he in these parts now?'

" 'Yes,' said the spaniel. 'We are staying at the Royal George. My master is painting some pictures of the country, and next week he is going back to London to commence the portrait of the prince.'

"Now, it happened that I had met this George Morland, who was, and is still, perhaps the most famous painter of farm-life pictures the world has ever known. I am proud to be able to say that I knew him. He was especially good at painting horses in stables, pigs in sties, roosters and dogs hanging around kitchen doors, and things like that.

"So, without letting the spaniel see that I was following him, I went after him, to see where he was going.

"He led me to a lonely old farm out on the hills. And

there, concealing myself in some bushes, I watched the great Morland painting one of his famous farm scenes.

"Presently he laid down his paintbrush and muttered to himself, 'I need a dog—by the watering trough there—to fill out the picture. I wonder if I could get that fool spaniel to lie still for five minutes . . . Here, Spot, Spot! Come here!'

"His spaniel, Spot, came up to him. And George, leaving his painting for a moment, placed the spaniel beside the watering trough and flattened him out and told him to keep still. I could see that George's idea was to have him look as though he were asleep in the sun. George simply loved to paint animals asleep in the sun.

"Well, that blockhead of a spaniel never kept still one minute. First, he was snapping at the flies that bit his tail; then he was scratching his ear, then barking at the cat— never still. And, of course, George couldn't paint him at all, and at last he got so angry he threw the paintbrush at him.

"Then an idea came to me—one of the best ideas I ever had. I left the bushes and came trotting up to George, wagging my tail. And how I thrilled with pride as the great Morland recognized me! For, mind you, he had met me only once before—back in the autumn of 1802.

"'Why, it's Jip!' he cried. 'Good dog. Come here. You're the very fellow I want.'"

"Then while he gathered up the things he had thrown at the spaniel he went on talking to me—the way people do talk to dogs, you know. Of course, he didn't expect me to understand what he said, but I did—every word.

"'I want you to come over here by the trough, Jip,' said he. 'All you've got to do is to keep still. You can go to sleep

" 'Come over here by the trough' "

if you like. But don't move or fidget for ten minutes. Think you can do that?'

"And he led me over to the trough, where I lay down and kept perfectly still while he painted me into the picture. That picture now hangs in the National Gallery. It's called *Evening on the Farm*. Hundreds of people go to see it every year. But none of them know that the smart-looking dog sleeping beneath the watering trough is none other than myself—except the Doctor, whom I took in to see it one day when we were up in London, shopping.

"Well, now, as I told you, I had an idea in all this. I hoped that if I did something for George Morland perhaps I could get him to do something for me. But, of course, with him not knowing dog talk it was a bit difficult to make him understand. However, while he was packing up his painting things I disappeared for a while, just as though I was going away. Then I came rushing back to him in a great state of excitement, barking, trying to show him something was wrong and that I wanted him to follow me.

" 'What's the matter, Jip?' said he. 'House on fire or something?'

"Then I barked some more and ran a little way in the direction of the town, looking back at him to show him I wanted him to come with me.

" 'What ails the dog?' he murmured to himself. 'Can't be anybody drowning because there's no river near . . . Oh, all right, Jip, I'll come. Wait a second till I get these brushes cleaned.'

"Then I led him into the town. On the way there every once in a while he would say to himself, 'I wonder what can be the matter. Something's wrong, that's sure, or the dog wouldn't carry on so.'

"I took him down the main street of the town till we came to the place where the beggar had his pictures. And as soon as George saw the pictures he *knew* what was wrong.

" 'Heaven preserve us!' he cried. 'What a dreadful exhibition! No wonder the dog was excited.'

"Well, it happened that as we came up the one-legged beggar, with his own dog beside him, was at work on a new drawing. He was sitting on the pavement, making a picture on canvas with a piece of chalk of a cat drinking milk. Now, my idea was that the great Morland—who, no matter what people say about him, was always a most kindhearted man—should make some good pictures for the beggar to show, instead of the dreadful messes that he made himself. And my plan worked.

" 'Man alive!' said George, pointing to the picture the beggar was doing, 'a cat's spine doesn't curve that way— here, give me the chalk and let me do it.'

"Then, rubbing out the whole picture, George Morland redrew it in his way. And it was so lifelike you could nearly hear the cat lapping up the milk.

" 'My! I wish I could draw that way,' said the beggar. 'And so quick and easy you do it—like it was nothing at all.'

" 'Well, it comes easy,' said George. 'Maybe there's not so much credit in it for that. But, tell me, do you make much money at this game?'

" 'Awful little,' said the beggar. 'I've taken only twopence the whole day. I suppose the truth is I don't draw good enough.'

"I watched Morland's face as the beggar said this. And the expression that came into it told me I had not brought the great man here in vain.

" 'Look here,' he said to the beggar. 'Would you like me to redraw all your pictures for you? Of course, those done on the pavement you couldn't sell, but we can rub them out. And I've got some spare canvases in my satchel here.

Maybe you could sell a few. I can sell pictures in London any day in the week. But I've never been a pavement artist before. It would be rather a lark to see what happens.'

"Then Morland, all busy and excited, like a schoolboy, took the beggar's chalk pictures from against the wall and, rubbing them out, did them over the way they should be done. He got so occupied with this that he didn't notice that a whole crowd of people was gathering around, watching. His work was so fine that the people were spellbound with the beauty of the cats and dogs and cows and horses that he drew. And they began asking one another in whispers who the stranger could be who was doing the pavement artist's pictures for him.

"The crowd grew bigger and bigger. And presently someone among the people who had seen Morland's pictures before recognized the work of the great artist. And then whispers went through the crowd: 'It's Morland, the great Morland himself.' And somebody went off and told a picture dealer—that is, a man who buys and sells pictures—who had a shop in the High Street, that George Morland was drawing in the marketplace for a lame beggar.

"And the dealer came down. And the mayor came down —and all the rich folk and poor folk. So, when the whole town was gathered around, the people began offering to buy these pictures, asking the beggar how much he wanted for them.

"The old duffer was going to sell them at sixpence apiece, but Morland whispered to him, 'Twenty guineas—don't sell a blessed one under twenty guineas. You'll get it.'

"And sure enough, the dealer and a few of the richer townsfolk bought the whole lot at twenty guineas apiece.

"And when I went home that night I felt I had done a good day's work. For my friend's master, the one-legged beggar, was now rich enough to live in comfort for the rest of his life."

· Chapter 7 ·

TOO-TOO'S STORY

All the animals had now told a story except Too-Too, the owl, and the pushmi-pullyu. And the following night, a Friday, it was agreed that they should toss a coin (the Doctor's penny that had a hole through it) to see which of these two should tell a tale. If the penny came down heads it was to be the pushmi-pullyu, and if it came down tails it was to be Too-Too's turn.

The Doctor tossed the penny and it came down tails.

"All right," said Too-Too. "Then that makes it my turn, I suppose. I will tell you a story of the time—the only time in my life—that I was taken for a fairy. Fancy me as a fairy!" chuckled the little round owl. "Well, this is how it happened: One October day, toward evening, I was wandering through the woods. There was a wintry tang in the air and the small, furred animals were busy among the dry, rustly leaves, gathering nuts and seeds for food against the coming of snow. I was out after shrew mice, myself—a delicacy I was extremely fond of at that time—

166

"The Doctor tossed the penny"

and while they were busy foraging they made easy hunting.

"In my travels through the woods I heard children's voices and the barking of a dog. Usually I would have gone farther into the forest, away from such sounds. But in my young days I was a curious bird and my curiosity often led me into many adventures. So instead of flying away, I went toward the noises I heard, moving cautiously from tree to tree so that I could see without being seen.

"Presently I came upon a children's picnic—several boys and girls having supper in a grove of oak trees. One boy, much larger than the rest, was teasing a dog. And two other children, a small girl and a small boy, were objecting to his cruelty and begging him to stop. The bully wouldn't stop. And soon the small boy and girl set upon him with their fists and feet and gave him quite a fine drubbing— which greatly surprised him. The dog then ran off home and presently the small boy and girl—I found out afterward they were brother and sister—wandered off from the rest of the picnicking party to look for mushrooms.

"I had admired their spirit greatly in punishing a boy so much bigger than they were. And when they wandered off by themselves, again out of curiosity, I followed them. Well, they traveled quite a distance for such small folk. And presently the sun set and darkness began to creep over the woods.

"Then the children thought to join their friends again and started back. But, being poor woodsmen, they took the wrong direction. It grew darker still, of course, as time went on, and soon the youngsters were tumbling and stumbling over roots they could not see and getting pretty thoroughly lost and tired.

"All this time I was following them secretly and noiselessly overhead. At last the children sat down and the little girl said, 'Willie, we're lost! Whatever shall we do? Night is coming on and I'm so afraid of the dark.'

"'So am I,' said the boy. 'Ever since Aunt Emily told us that spooky story of the "Bogey in the Cupboard," I've been scared to death of the dark.'

"Well, you could have knocked me down with a feather. Of course, you must realize that was the first time I had ever heard of anyone's being afraid of the dark. It sounds ridiculous enough to all of you, I suppose, but to me, who had always preferred the cool, calm darkness to the glaring, vulgar daylight, it seemed then an almost unbelievable thing that anyone could be afraid merely because the sun had gone to bed.

"Now, some people have an idea that bats and owls can see in the dark because we have some peculiar kind of eyes. It's not so. Peculiar ears we have—but not eyes. We can see in the dark because we practice it. It's all a matter of practice—the same as the piano or anything else. We get up when other people go to bed, and go to bed when other people get up, because we prefer the dark; and you'd be surprised how much nicer it is when you get used to it. Of course, we owls are specially trained by our mothers and fathers to see on very dark nights when we are quite young. So it comes easier to us. But anybody can do it—to a certain extent—if they only practice.

"Well, to return to the children: There they were, all fussed and worried and scared, sitting on the ground, weeping and wondering what they could do. Then, remembering the dog and knowing they were kind to animals, I thought I would try to help them. So I popped across into the tree over their heads and said in the kindliest, gentlest sort of a voice, *Too-wit, Too-hoo!*—which means in owl language, as you know, 'It's a fine night! How are you?'

"Then you should have seen those poor children jump!

" 'Ugh!' says the little girl, clutching her brother around the neck. 'What was that, a spook?'

" 'I don't know,' says the little boy. 'Gosh, but I'm scared! Isn't the dark awful?'

" 'What was that?' "

"Then I made two or three more attempts to comfort them, talking kindly to them in owl language. But they only grew scareder and scareder. First they thought I was a bogey, then an ogre, then a giant of the forest—me, whom they could put in their pockets! Golly, but these human creatures do bring up their children in awful ignorance! If there ever was a bogey or a giant or an ogre—in the forest or out of it—I've yet to see one.

"Then I thought maybe if I went off through the woods

too-witting and too-hooing all the way, they would follow me and I could then lead them out of the forest and show them the way home. So I tried it. But they didn't follow me, the stupid little beggars—thinking I was a witch or some evil nonsense of that kind. And all I got for my too-witting and too-hooing all over the place was to wake up another owl some distance off, who thought I was calling to him.

"So, since I wasn't doing the children any good, I went off to look up this other owl and see if he had any ideas to suggest. I found him sitting on the stump of a hollow birch, rubbing his eyes, having just gotten out of bed.

" 'Good evening,' says I. 'It's a fine night!'

" 'It is,' says he, 'only it's not dark enough. What were you making all that racket over there for just now? Waking a fellow out of his sleep before it's gotten properly dark!'

" 'I'm sorry,' I said, 'but there's a couple of children over in the hollow there who've gotten lost. The little silly duffers are sitting on the ground, bawling because the daylight's gone and they don't know what to do.'

" 'My gracious!' says he. 'What a quaint notion. Why don't you lead them out of the woods? They probably live over in one of those farms near the crossroads.'

" 'I've tried,' I said. 'But they're so scared they won't follow me. They don't like my voice, or something. They take me for a wicked ogre, and all that sort of rot.'

" 'Well,' says he, 'then you'll have to give an imitation of some other kind of creature—one they're not scared of. Are you any good at imitations? Can you bark like a dog?'

" 'No,' I said. 'But I can make a noise like a cat. I learned that from an American catbird that lived in a cage in the stable where I spent last summer.'

" 'Fine,' says he. 'Try that and see what happens!'

"So I went back to the children and found them weeping harder than ever. Then, keeping myself well hidden down near the ground among the bushes, I went, *Meow! Me-o-w!'* real catlike.

" 'Oh, Willie,' says the little girl to her brother, 'we're saved!' ('Saved,' mark you, when neither of the boobies was in the slightest danger!) 'We're saved!' says she. 'There's Tuffie, our cat, come for us. She'll show us the way home. Cats can always find their way home, can't they, Willie? Let's follow her!' "

For a moment Too-Too's plump sides shook with silent laughter as he recalled the scene he was describing.

"Then," said he, "I went a little farther off, still taking great care that I shouldn't be seen, and I meowed again.

" 'There she is!' said the little girl. 'She's calling to us. Come along, Willie.'

"Well, in that way, keeping ahead of them and calling like a cat, I finally led the children right out of the woods. They did a good deal of stumbling and the girl's long hair often got caught in the bushes. But I always waited for them if they were lagging behind. At last, when we gained the open fields, we saw three houses on the skyline, and the middle one was all lighted up and people with lanterns were running around it, hunting in all directions.

"When I had brought the children right up to this house their mother and father made a tremendous fuss, weeping over them as though they had been saved from some terrible danger. In my opinion grown-up humans are even more stupid than the young ones. You'd think, from the way that mother and father carried on, that those children had been wrecked on a desert island, or something, instead of spending a couple of hours in the pleasant woods.

" 'How ever did you find your way, Willie?' asked the mother, wiping away her tears and smiling all over.

" 'Tuffie brought us home,' says the little girl. 'She came out after us and led us here by going ahead of us and meowing.'

" '*Tuffie!*' says the mother, puzzled. 'Why, the cat's asleep in the parlor in front of the fire—been there all evening.'

" 'Well, it was some cat,' says the boy. 'He must be right around here somewhere because he led us almost up to the door.'

"Then the father swings his lantern around, looking for a cat; and before I had time to hop away he throws the light full on me, sitting on a sage bush.

" 'Why, it's an *owl!*' cries the little girl.

" '*Meow!*' says I—just to show off. *'Too-wit, Too-hoo! Meow! Meow!'* And with a farewell flip of the wing I disappeared into the night over the barn roof.

"But as I left I heard the little girl saying in tremendous excitement, 'Oh, Mother, a fairy! It was a fairy that brought us home. It must have been—disguised as an owl! At last! At last I've seen a fairy!'

"Well, that's the first and last time I ever expect to be taken for a fairy. But I got to know those children quite well. They were a real nice couple of kiddies—even if the little girl did keep on insisting that I was a fairy in disguise. I used to hang around their barn, nights, looking for mice and rats. But if those youngsters ever caught sight of me they'd follow me everywhere. After bringing them safely home that evening I could have led them across the Sahara Desert and they'd follow—certain in their minds that I was the best of all good fairies and would keep them out of harm. They used to bring me mutton chops and shrimps and all the best tidbits from their parents' table. And I lived like a fighting cock—got so fat and lazy I couldn't have caught a mouse on crutches.

"They were never afraid of the dark again. Because, you see—as I said to the Doctor one day, when we were talking over the multiplication tables and other philosophy—fear is usually ignorance. Once you know a thing, you're no longer afraid of it. And those youngsters got to know the dark—and then they saw, of course, that it was just as harmless as the day.

"I used to take them out into the woods at night and across the hills and they got to love it—liked the adventure, you know. And thinking it would be a good thing if some humans, anyway, had sense enough to travel without sunlight, I taught them how to see in the dark. They soon got on to it, when they saw how I always shaded my eyes in the light of a lantern, so as not to get the habit of strong light. Well, those young ones became real expert—not so good as an owl or a bat, of course, but quite good at seeing in the dark for anyone who had not been brought up that way.

"It came in handy for them, too. That part of the country got flooded one springtime in the middle of the night and there wasn't a dry match or a light to be had anywhere. Then those children, who had traveled all that country scores of times in the dark with me, saved a great many lives. They acted as guides, you understand, and took the people to safety because they knew how to use their eyes, and the others didn't."

Too-Too yawned and blinked up sleepily at the lantern hanging above his head.

"Seeing in the dark," he ended, "is all a matter of practice—same as the piano or anything else."

The next night it came at last to the pushmi-pullyu's turn for a story. But he was very shy and modest and when the animals asked him the following night he said in his very well-bred manner, "I'm terribly sorry to disappoint you, but I'm afraid I don't know any stories—at least none good enough to entertain you with."

"Oh, come on, Push," said Jip. "Don't be so bashful. We've all told one. You don't mean to say you've lived all your life in the African jungle without seeing any adventures? There must be lots of yarns you could tell us."

"But I've mostly led such a quiet life, you see," said the pushmi-pullyu. "Our people have always kept very much to themselves. We mind our own business and don't like getting mixed up in scandals and rows and adventures."

"Oh, we'll let him pass this time," said Dab-Dab. "Don't press him into it if he's too shy."

Everybody had now told a tale and the *Arctic Monthly*'s prize-story competition was declared closed. The first number of the first animals' magazine ever printed was, shortly after that, issued and circulated by Swallow Mail to the inhabitants of the frozen north. It was a great success. Letters of thanks and votes on the competition began pouring in from seals and sea lions and caribou and all manner of polar creatures. Too-Too, the mathematician, became editor; Dab-Dab ran the mothers' and babies' page, while

Gub-Gub wrote the gardening notes and the pure-foods column. And the *Arctic Monthly* continued to bring happiness to homes and dens and icebergs as long as the Doctor's post office existed.

PART FOUR

· Chapter 1 ·
PARCEL POST

One day Gub-Gub came to the Doctor and said, "Doctor, why don't you start a parcel post?"

"Great heavens, Gub-Gub!" the Doctor exclaimed. "Don't you think I'm busy enough already? What do you want a parcel post for?"

"I'll bet it's something to do with food," said Too-Too, who was sitting on the stool next to the Doctor's, adding up figures.

"Well," said Gub-Gub, "I was thinking of sending to England for some fresh vegetables."

"There you are!" said Too-Too. "He has a vegetable mind."

"But parcels would be too heavy for the birds to carry, Gub-Gub," said the Doctor, "except perhaps the small parcels by the bigger birds."

"Yes, I know. I had thought of that," said the pig. "But this month the brussels sprouts will be coming into season in England. They're my favorite vegetable, you know—after parsnips. And I hear that a special kind of thrushes will be leaving England next week to come to Africa. It wouldn't be too much to ask them to bring a single brussels sprout apiece, would it? There will be hundreds of birds in the flight and if they each brought a sprout we'd have enough to last us for months. I haven't tasted any fresh English vegetables since last autumn, Doctor. And I'm so sick of these yams and okras and other rubbish."

"All right, Gub-Gub," said the Doctor, "I'll see what I can do. We will send a letter to England by the next mail going out and ask the thrushes to bring you your brussels sprouts."

Well, that was how still another department, the parcel post, was added to the foreign mails office of Fantippo. Gub-Gub's sprouts arrived (tons of them, because this was a very big flight of birds), and after that many kinds of animals came to the Doctor and asked him to send for foreign foods for them when their own ran short. In this way, too, bringing seeds and plants from other lands by birds, the Doctor tried quite a number of experiments in planting, and what is called acclimatizing, fruits and vegetables and even flowers.

And very soon he had an old-fashioned window-box garden on the houseboat post office blooming with geraniums and marigolds and zinnias raised from the seeds and cuttings his birds brought him from England.

A little while after that, by using the larger birds to carry packages, a regular parcel post every two months was put at the service of the Fantippans; and alarm clocks and all sorts of things from England were sent for.

King Koko even sent for a new bicycle. It was brought over in pieces—two storks carrying a wheel each; an eagle the frame; and crows the smaller parts, such as the pedals, the spanners, and the oil can.

When they started to put it together again in the post office, a part—one of the nuts—was found to be missing. But that was not the fault of the parcel post. It had been left out by the makers, who shipped it from Birmingham. But the Doctor wrote a letter of complaint by the next mail and a new nut was sent right away. Then the King rode triumphantly through the streets of Fantippo on his new bicycle and a public holiday was held in honor of the occasion. And he gave his old bicycle to his brother, Prince Wolla-Bolla. And the parcel post, which had really been started by Gub-Gub, was declared a great success.

Some weeks later the Doctor received this letter from a farmer in Lincolnshire:

Dear Sir:

Thank you for your excellent weather reports. By their help I managed to raise the finest crop of brussels sprouts this year ever seen in Lincolnshire. But the night before I was going to pick them for market they disappeared from my fields—every blessed one of them. How, I don't know. Maybe you could give me some advice about this.

Your obedient servant,
Nicholas Scroggins

"Great heavens!" said the Doctor. "I wonder what happened to them."

"Gub-Gub ate them," said Too-Too. "Those are the sprouts, no doubt, that the thrushes brought here."

"Dear me!" said the Doctor. "That's too bad. Well, I daresay I'll find some way to pay the farmer back."

For a long time Dab-Dab, the motherly housekeeper, had

been trying to get the Doctor to take a holiday from his post-office business.

"You know, Doctor," said she, "you're going to get sick— that's what's going to happen to you, as sure as you're alive. No man can work the way you've been doing for the last few months and not pay for it. Now that you've got the post office going properly, why don't you hand it over to the King's postmen to run and give yourself a rest? And, anyway, aren't you ever going back to Puddleby?"

"Oh, yes," said John Dolittle. "All in good time, Dab-Dab."

"But you *must* take a holiday," the duck insisted. "Get away from the post office for a while. Go up the coast in a canoe for a change of air—if you won't go home."

Well, the Doctor kept saying that he would go. But he never did—until something happened to take him from his post-office work. This is how it came about:

One day the Doctor was opening the mail addressed to him, when he came upon a package about the size and shape of a large egg. He undid the outer wrapper, which was made of seaweed. Inside he found a letter and a pair of oyster shells tied together like a box.

Somewhat puzzled, the Doctor first read the letter, while Dab-Dab, who was still badgering him about taking a holiday, looked over his shoulder. The letter said:

Dear Doctor:

I am sending you, enclosed, some pretty pebbles that I found the other day while cracking open oysters. I never saw pebbles of this color before, though I live by the seashore and have been opening shellfish all my life. My husband says they're oysters' eggs. But I don't believe it.

"Dab-Dab looked over his shoulder"

Would you please tell me what they are? And be careful to send them back because my children use them as playthings, and I have promised them they shall have them to keep.

Then the Doctor put down the letter and, taking his penknife, he cut the seaweed strings that neatly held the oyster shells together. And when he opened the shells he gave a gasp of astonishment.

"Oh, Dab-Dab," he cried, "how beautiful! Look, look!"

"Pearls!" whispered Dab-Dab in an awed voice, gazing down into the Doctor's palm. "Pink pearls!"

"My! Aren't they handsome?" murmured the Doctor. "And did you ever see such large ones? Each one of those pearls, Dab-Dab, is worth a fortune. Who the dickens is this that sent them to me, anyhow?"

And he turned to the letter again.

"It's from a spoonbill," said Dab-Dab. "I know their writing. They are a sort of a cross between a curlew and a snipe. They like messing around lonely seacoast places, hunting for shellfish and sea worms and stuff like that."

"Well, where is it written from?" asked the Doctor. "What do you make that address out to be—at the top of the page there?"

Dab-Dab screwed up her eyes and peered at it closely.

"It looks to me," she said, "like the Harmattan Rocks."

"Where is that?" asked the Doctor.

"I have no idea," said Dab-Dab. "But Speedy will know."

And she went off to fetch the Skimmer.

Speedy said, yes, he knew—the Harmattan Rocks were a group of small islands off the coast of West Africa, about sixty miles farther to the northward.

"That's curious," said the Doctor. "I wouldn't have been so surprised if they had come from the South Sea Islands. But it is rather unusual to find pearls of any size or beauty in these waters. Well, these must be sent back to the spoonbill's children—by registered parcel post, of course. Though, to tell you the truth, I hate to part with them— they are so lovely. They can't go before tomorrow, anyway. I wonder where I can keep them in the meantime. One has to be frightfully careful with gems as valuable as these.

You had better not tell anyone about them, Dab-Dab—except Jip, the watchman, and the pushmi-pullyu. They must take it in turns to mount guard at the door all night. Men will do all sorts of things for pearls. We'll keep it a secret and send them right back first thing tomorrow morning."

Even while the Doctor was speaking he noticed a shadow fall across the desk at which he was standing. He looked up. And there at the information window was the ugliest man's face he had ever seen, staring in at the beautiful pearls that still lay on the palm of his hand.

The Doctor, annoyed and embarrassed, forgot for the first time in his post-office career to be polite.

"What do *you* want?" he asked, thrusting the pearls into his pocket.

"I want a postal order for ten shillings," said the man. "I am going to send some money to my sick wife."

The Doctor made out the postal order and took the money, which the man handed through the window.

"Here you are," he said.

Then the man left the post office and the Doctor watched him go.

"That was a queer-looking customer, wasn't he?" he said to Dab-Dab.

"He was, indeed," said the duck. "I'm not surprised his wife is sick, if she has a husband with a face like that."

"I wonder who he is," said John Dolittle. "It isn't often we have strangers coming in here. I don't much like the looks of him."

The following day the pearls were wrapped up again the way they had arrived, and after a letter had been written by the Doctor explaining to the spoonbill what the "pebbles" really were, they were sent off by registered parcel post to the Harmattan Rocks.

The bird chosen to take the package happened to be one of the thrushes that had brought the brussels sprouts from England. These birds were still staying in the neighborhood. And though a thrush was a somewhat small bird to carry parcel post, the package was a very little one and the Doctor had nobody else to send. So after explaining to the thrush that registered mail should be guarded very carefully by postmen, the Doctor sent the pearls off.

Then he went to call on the King, as he did every so often. And in the course of conversation John Dolittle asked His Majesty if he knew who the stranger might be that had called at the houseboat for a postal order.

After he had listened to the description of the man's cross-eyed, ugly face, the King said, yes, he knew him very well. He was a pearl fisherman, who spent most of his time in the Pacific Ocean, where fishing for pearls was more common. But, the King said, he often came hanging around these parts, where he was known to be a great villain who would do anything to get pearls or money. Jack Wilkins was his name.

The Doctor, on hearing this, felt glad that he had already got the pink pearls safely off to their owner by registered mail. Then he told the King that he hoped shortly to take a holiday because he was overworked and needed a rest. The King asked where he was going, and the Doctor said he thought of taking a week's canoe trip up the coast toward the Harmattan Rocks.

"Well," said His Majesty, "if you are going in that direction you might call on an old friend of mine, Chief Nyam-Nyam. He owns the country in those parts and the

Harmattan Rocks themselves. He and his people are frightfully poor, though. But he is honest—and I think you will like him."

"All right," said the Doctor, "I'll call on him with your compliments."

The next day, leaving Speedy, Cheapside, and Jip in charge of the post office, the Doctor got into his canoe with Dab-Dab and paddled off to take his holiday. On the way out he noticed a schooner, the ship of Jack Wilkins, the pearl fisherman, at anchor near the entrance to Fantippo harbor.

Toward evening the Doctor arrived at a small settlement of straw huts, the village of Chief Nyam-Nyam. Calling on the chief with an introduction from King Koko, the Doctor was well received. He found, however, that the country over which this chief ruled was indeed in a very poor state. For years powerful neighbors on either side had made war on the old chief and robbed him of his best farming lands, till now his people were crowded onto a narrow strip of rocky shore where very little food could be grown. The Doctor was particularly distressed by the thinness of the few chickens pecking about in the streets. They reminded him of old broken-down cab horses, he said.

While he was talking to the chief (who seemed to be a kindly old man) Speedy swept into the chief's hut in a great state of excitement.

"Doctor," he cried, "the mail has been robbed! The thrush has come back to the post office and says his package was taken from him on the way. *The pearls are gone!*"

· Chapter 2 ·

THE GREAT MAIL ROBBERY

reat heavens!" cried the Doctor, springing up. "The pearls gone? And they were registered, too!"

"Yes," said Speedy, "here's the thrush himself. He'll tell you all about it."

And going to the door, he called in the bird who had carried the registered package.

"Doctor," said the thrush, who was also very upset and breathless, "it wasn't my fault. I never let those pearls out of my sight. I flew straight off for the Harmattan Rocks. But part of the trip I had to go over land, if I took the shortest cut. And on the way I saw a sister of mine, whom I hadn't met in a long time, sitting in a tree in the jungle below me. And I thought it would be no harm if I went and talked to her a while. So I flew down and she was very glad to see me. I couldn't talk properly with the string of the package in my mouth, so I put the parcel down on the bough of the tree behind me—right near me, you under-

" 'I put the parcel down' "

stand—and went on talking to my sister. And when I
turned around to pick it up again it was gone."

"Perhaps it slipped off the tree," said the Doctor, "and
fell down into the underbrush."

"It couldn't have," said the thrush. "I put it into a little
hollow in the bark of the bough. It just couldn't have
slipped or rolled. Somebody must have taken it."

"Dear me," said John Dolittle. "Robbing the mails—
that's a serious thing. I wonder who could have done it?"

"I'll bet it's Jack Wilkins, the cross-eyed pearl fisherman," whispered Dab-Dab. "A man with a face like that would steal anything. And he was the only one, besides us and Speedy, who knew the pearls were going through the mails. It's Wilkins, sure as you're alive."

"I wonder," said the Doctor. "They do say he is a most unscrupulous customer. Well, there's nothing for it, I suppose, but that I should paddle back to Fantippo right away and try to find him. The post office is responsible for the loss of registered mail, and if Mr. Wilkins took those pearls I'm going to get them back again. But after this we will make it a post-office rule that carriers of registered mail may not talk to their sisters or anyone else while on duty."

And in spite of the lateness of the hour, John Dolittle said a hasty farewell to Chief Nyam-Nyam and started off by moonlight for Fantippo harbor.

In the meantime, Speedy and the thrush flew over the land by the shortcut to the post office.

"What are you going to say to Wilkins, Doctor?" asked Dab-Dab as the canoe glided along over the moonlit sea. "It's a pity you haven't got a pistol or something like that. He looks like a desperate character, and he isn't likely to give up the pearls without a fight."

"I don't know what I'll say to him. I'll see when I get there," said John Dolittle. "But we must be very careful how we approach, so that he doesn't see us coming. If he should pull up his anchor and sail away, we would never be able to overtake him by canoe."

"I tell you what, Doctor," said Dab-Dab, "let me fly ahead and do a little spying on the enemy. Then I'll come back and tell you anything I can find out. Maybe he isn't on his schooner at all at present, and we ought to be hunting him somewhere else."

"All right," said the Doctor. "Do that. It will take me another four hours at least to reach Fantippo at this pace."

So Dab-Dab flew away over the sea and John Dolittle continued to paddle his canoe bravely forward.

After about an hour had passed he heard a gentle sort of whispered quacking high overhead and he knew that his faithful housekeeper was returning. Presently, with a swish of feathers, Dab-Dab settled down at his feet. And on her face was an expression that meant great news.

"He's there, Doctor—and he's got the pearls, all right!" said she. "I peeked through the window and I saw him counting them out from one little box into another by the light of a candle."

"The villain!" grunted the Doctor, putting on all the speed he could. "Let's hope he doesn't get away before we reach Fantippo."

Dawn was beginning to show before they came in sight of the ship they sought. This made approaching the schooner without being seen extremely difficult. And the Doctor went all the way around the island of No-Man's-Land, so as to come upon the ship from the other side, where he would not have to cross so large an open stretch of sea.

Paddling very, very softly, he managed to get the canoe right under the bow of the ship. Then, tying his own craft so it couldn't float away, he swarmed up the schooner's anchor chain and crept on to the boat on hands and knees.

Full daylight had not yet come and the light from a lamp could be seen palely shining up the stairs that led to the

HUGH LOFTING

"Wilkins leveled a pistol at the Doctor's head"

cabin. The Doctor slid forward like a shadow, tiptoed his way down the stairs and peered through the partly opened door.

The cross-eyed Wilkins was still seated at the table, as Dab-Dab had described, counting pearls. Two other men were asleep in bunks around the room. The Doctor swung open the door and jumped in. Instantly Wilkins sprang up from the table, snatched a pistol from his belt and leveled it at the Doctor's head.

"Move an inch and you're a dead man!" he snarled.

The Doctor, taken aback for a moment, gazed at the pistol muzzle, wondering what to do next. Wilkins, without moving his eyes from the Doctor for a second, closed the pearl box with his left hand and put it into his pocket.

While he was doing this, however, Dab-Dab sneaked in under the table, unseen by anyone. And suddenly she bit the pearl fisherman in the leg with her powerful beak.

With a howl Wilkins bent down to knock her off.

"Now's your chance, Doctor!" yelled the duck.

And in the second while the pistol was lowered the Doctor sprang onto the man's back, gripped him around the neck, and with a crash the two of them went rolling on the floor of the cabin.

Then a tremendous fight began. Over and over and over they rolled around the floor, upsetting things in all directions, Wilkins fighting to get his pistol hand free, the Doctor struggling to keep it bound to his body, Dab-Dab hopping and flying and jumping and flapping to get a bite in on the enemy's nose whenever she saw a chance.

At last John Dolittle, who for his size, was a very powerful wrestler, got the pearl fisherman in a grip of iron where he couldn't move at all. But just as the Doctor was forcing the pistol out of his enemy's hand, one of the other men, who had been aroused by the noise of the fight, woke up. And, leaning out of his bunk from behind the Doctor's back, he hit him a tremendous blow on the head with a bottle. Stunned and senseless, John Dolittle fell over in a heap and lay still upon the floor.

Then all three men sprang on him with ropes and in a minute his arms and legs were tied, and the fight was over.

* * *

When he woke up the Doctor found himself lying at the bottom of his own canoe, with Dab-Dab tugging at the ropes that bound his wrists to get him free.

"Where is Wilkins?" he asked in a dazed, sleepy kind of way.

"Gone," said Dab-Dab; "and the pearls with him—the scoundrel! As soon as they had dumped you in the canoe they pulled up the anchor, hoisted sail, and got away. They were in an awful hurry and kept looking out to sea with telescopes and talking about the revenue cutter. I guess they are wanted by the government for a good many bad deeds. I never saw a tougher-looking crowd of men in all my life. See, I've got the rope around your hands free now; you can do the rest better yourself. Does your head hurt much?"

"It's a bit dizzy still," said the Doctor, working at the rope about his ankles. "But I'll be all right in a little."

Presently when he had undone the cord that tied his feet, John Dolittle stood up and gazed over the ocean. And there, on the skyline, he could just see the sails of Wilkins's schooner disappearing eastward.

"Villain!" was all he said between his clenched teeth.

· Chapter 3 ·

PEARLS AND BRUSSELS SPROUTS

Disappointed and sad, Dab-Dab and the Doctor
started to paddle their way back.

"I think I'll stop in at the post office before I return to
Chief Nyam-Nyam's country," said the Doctor. "There's
nothing more I can do about the pearls, I suppose. But I'd
like to see if everything else is going all right."

"Wilkins may get caught yet—by the government," said
Dab-Dab. "And if he does, we might get the pearls back,
after all."

"Not much chance of that, I'm afraid," said John Dolittle. "He will probably sell them the first chance he gets.
That's all he wants them for—for the money they'll bring
in. Whereas the young spoonbills appreciated their beauty.
It's a shame they should lose them—and when they were
in my care, too. Well—it's no use crying over spilled milk.
They're gone. That's all."

As they were approaching the houseboat they noticed a
large number of canoes collected about it. Today was not

195

one of the outgoing or incoming mail days and the Doctor wondered what the excitement could be.

Fastening up his own canoe, he went into the post office. And inside there was quite a crowd. He made his way through it with Dab-Dab and in the registered-mail booth he found all the animals gathered around a small black squirrel. The little creature's legs were tied with post-office red tape, and he seemed very frightened and miserable. Speedy and Cheapside were mounting guard over him, one on each side.

"What's all this about?" asked the Doctor.

"We've caught the fellow who stole the pearls, Doctor," said Speedy.

"And we've got the pearls, too," cried Too-Too. "They're in the stamp drawer, and Jip is guarding them."

"But I don't understand," said John Dolittle. "I thought Wilkins had made off with them."

"Those must have been some other stolen pearls, Doctor," said Dab-Dab. "Let's take a look at the ones Jip has."

The Doctor went and opened the stamp drawer. And there, inside, sure enough, were the three pink beauties he had sent by registered mail.

"How did you find them?" he asked, turning to Speedy.

"Well, after you had set off in the canoe," said the Skimmer, "I and the thrush stopped on our way back here at the tree where he had lost the package. It was too dark then to hunt for it, so we roosted in the tree all night, intending to look in the morning. Just as dawn was breaking, we saw this wretched squirrel here flirting about in the branches with an enormous pink pearl in his mouth. I at once pounced on him and held him down, while the thrush took the pearl away from him. Then we made him tell us where he had hidden the other two. And after we had gotten all three of them we put the squirrel under arrest and brought him here."

"Dear me!" said the Doctor, looking at the miserable culprit, who was all tied up with red tape. "What made you steal the pearls?"

At first the squirrel seemed almost too frightened to speak. So the Doctor took a pair of scissors and cut the bonds that held him.

"Why did you do it?" he repeated.

"I thought they were brussels sprouts," said the squirrel timidly. "A few weeks ago when I and my wife were sitting in a tree we suddenly smelled the smell of brussels sprouts, awful strong, all about us. I and my wife are very fond of this vegetable and we wondered where the smell was coming from. And then, looking up, we saw thousands of thrushes passing overhead, carrying brussels sprouts in their mouths. We hoped they would stop so we could get a few. But they didn't. So we agreed that perhaps more would be coming over in a few days. And we arranged to stay around that same tree and wait. And, sure enough, this morning I saw one of these same thrushes alight in the tree, carrying a package. *'Pst!'* I whispered to the wife. 'More brussels sprouts. Let's bag his parcel while he's not looking!' And bag it I did. But when we opened it we found nothing but these wretched gewgaws. I thought they might be some new kind of rock candy and I was on my way to find a stone to crack them with, when this bird grabbed me by the scruff of the neck and arrested me. I didn't want the beastly pearls."

"Well," said the Doctor, "I'm sorry you've been put to such inconvenience. I'll have Dab-Dab carry you back to

" *'Pst!'* I whispered to the wife"

your family. But, you know, robbing the registered mail is a serious thing. If you wanted some brussels sprouts you should have written to me. After all, you can't blame the birds for putting you under arrest."

"Stolen fruit's the sweetest, Doctor," said Cheapside. "If you 'ad given 'im a ton of 'ot'ouse grapes 'e wouldn't 'ave enjoyed 'em 'alf as much as something 'e pinched. I'd give 'im a couple of years 'ard labor, if I was you—just to learn 'im to leave the mails alone."

"Well, never mind. We'll forget it," said the Doctor. "It's only a boyish escapade."

"Boyish, fiddlesticks!" growled Cheapside. " 'E's the father of a large family—and a natural-born pickpocket. All squirrels are like that. Don't I know 'em in the city parks—with their mincin' ways that the folks call 'cute'? Cheekiest beggars that ever was—pinch a crumb from under your nose and pop into an 'ole with it before you could get your breath. Boyish hescapade!"

"Come along," said Dab-Dab, picking the wretched culprit up in her big webbed feet. "I'll take you back to the mainland. And you can thank your lucky stars that it's the Doctor who is in charge of this post office. It's to jail you really ought to go."

"Oh, and hurry back, Dab-Dab," the Doctor called after her as she flapped her way through the open window and set off across the sea with her burden. "I'm going to start right away for Chief Nyam-Nyam's country as soon as you are ready."

"I'll take the pearls myself this time," he said to Speedy, "and hand them over to the spoonbill in person. We don't want any more accidents happening to them."

About noon the Doctor started out a second time upon his holiday trip and as Gub-Gub, Jip and the white mouse begged to be taken along, the canoe was well loaded.

They reached Nyam-Nyam's village about six o'clock in the evening and the old chief prepared a supper for his guests. There was very little to eat at it, however. And the Doctor was again reminded how poor these people were.

While talking with the old chief the Doctor found out that the worst enemy his country had was the Kingdom of Dahomey. This big and powerful neighbor was, it seemed, always making war upon Chief Nyam-Nyam and cutting off parts of his land and making the people poorer still. Now, the soldiers of Dahomey were Amazons—that is, they were women soldiers. And although they were women, they were very big and strong and there were a terrible lot of them. So whenever they attacked the small country next to them, they easily won and took what they wanted.

As it happened, they made an attack that night while the Doctor was staying with the chief. And about ten o'clock everybody was awakened out of his sleep with cries of "War! War! The Amazons are here!"

There was terrible confusion. And until the moon had risen people were hitting and falling over one another everywhere in the darkness, not knowing friend from enemy.

When it was possible to see, however, the Doctor found that most of Chief Nyam-Nyam's people had fled off into the jungle; and the Amazons, in thousands, were just going through the village, taking anything they fancied. The Doctor tried to argue with them, but they merely laughed at him.

Then the white mouse, who was watching the show from the Doctor's shoulder, whispered in his ear, "If this is an army of women, Doctor, I think I know of a way to deal with them. Women are terribly afraid of mice, you know. I'll just go off and collect a few in the village and see what we can do."

So the white mouse went off and gathered an army of his own, about two hundred mice, which lived in the grass walls and floors of the huts. And then suddenly they attacked the Amazons and began nipping them in the legs.

With shrieks and howls the fat women soldiers dropped the things they had been stealing and ran helter-skelter for home. And that was one time the famous Amazons of Dahomey *didn't* have it all their own way.

The Doctor told his pet he could be very proud of himself. For he was surely the only mouse in the world that ever won a war.

· Chapter 4 ·

PEARL DIVERS

The next morning the Doctor was up early. After a light breakfast (it was impossible to get any other kind in that poverty-stricken country) he asked Nyam-Nyam the way to the Harmattan Rocks and the chief told him they were about an hour and a half's paddle straight out into the ocean.

So the Doctor decided that he had better have a seabird to guide him. And Dab-Dab went and got a curlew who was strolling about on the beach, doing nothing in particular. This bird said he knew the place quite well and would consider it an honor to act as guide to John Dolittle. Then, with Jip, Dab-Dab, Gub-Gub, and the white mouse, the Doctor got into his canoe and started off for the Harmattan Rocks.

It was a beautiful morning and they enjoyed the paddle —though Gub-Gub came very near to upsetting the canoe more than once, leaning out to grab for passing seaweed, which he had noticed the curlew eating. Finally, for safety's sake, they made him lie down at the bottom of the canoe, where he couldn't see anything.

About eleven o'clock a group of little rocky islands were sighted, which their guide said were the Harmattan Rocks. At this point in their journey the mainland of Africa was just disappearing from view on the skyline behind them. The rocks they were coming to seemed to be the home of thousands of different kinds of seabirds. As the canoe drew near, gulls, terns, gannets, albatrosses, cormorants, auklets, petrels, wild ducks, even wild geese, came out, full of curiosity to examine the stranger. When they learned from the curlew that this quiet little fat man was none other than the great Doctor Dolittle himself, they passed word back to the rocks; and soon the air about the canoe was simply thick with wings flashing in the sunlight. And the welcome to their home that the seabirds screeched to the Doctor was so hearty and noisy you couldn't hear yourself speak.

It was easy to see why this place had been chosen for a home by the seabirds. The shores all around were guarded by half-sunken rocks, on which the waves roared and broke dangerously. No ship was ever likely to come here to disturb the quiet life of the birds. Indeed, even with a light canoe that could go in shallow water, the Doctor would have had hard work to make a landing. But the welcoming birds guided him very skillfully around to the back of the biggest island, where a bay with deep water formed a pretty sort of toy harbor. The Doctor understood now why these islands had been left in the possession of the poor chief: no neighbors would consider them worth taking. Hard to approach, with very little soil in which crops could be grown, flat and open to all the winds and gales of heaven, barren and lonesome, they tempted none of the chief's enemies. And so for many, many years they remained the property of Nyam-Nyam and his people— though indeed even they hardly ever visited them. But in the end, the Harmattan Rocks proved to be of greater value than all the rest of the lands this tribe had lost.

"Oh, I think this is an awful place," said Gub-Gub as they got out of the canoe. "Nothing but waves and rocks. What have you come here for, Doctor?"

"I hope to do a little pearl fishing," said John Dolittle. "But first I must see the spoonbill and give her this registered package. Dab-Dab, would you please try to find her for me? With so many millions of seabirds around, myself, I wouldn't know how to begin to look for her."

"All right," said Dab-Dab. "But it may take me a little time. There are several islands and quite a number of spoonbills. I shall have to make inquiries and find out which one sent you the pearls."

So Dab-Dab went off upon her errand. The birds, who at first followed the Doctor in droves around the main island wherever he went, presently returned to their ordinary doings when the newness of his arrival had worn off. And after Dab-Dab had come back from her hunt and told him the spoonbill lived on one of the smaller islands, he got back into his canoe and paddled over to the rock she pointed out.

Here the spoonbill was waiting for him at the water's edge. She apologized for not coming in person to welcome him, but said she was afraid to leave her babies when there were sea eagles around. The little ones were with her, two scrubby, greasy youngsters, who could walk but not fly. The Doctor opened the package and gave them back their

" 'Oh, I think this is an awful place!' "

precious toys; and with squawks of delight they began playing marbles on the flat rocks with the enormous pink pearls.

"What charming children you have," said the Doctor to the mother spoonbill, who was watching them proudly. "I'm glad they've got their playthings safely back. I wouldn't have had them lose them for anything."

"Yes, they are devoted to those pebbles," said the spoon-

"The young ones were with her"

bill. "By the way, were you able to tell me what they are? I found them, as I wrote you, inside an oyster."

"They are pearls," said the Doctor, "and worth a tremendous lot. Ladies in cities wear them around their necks."

"Oh, indeed," said the bird. "And why don't the ladies in the country wear them, too?"

"I just don't know," said the Doctor. "I suppose because they're too costly. With any one of those pearls you could buy a house and garden."

"Well, wouldn't you like to keep them, then?" asked the spoonbill. "I could get the children something else to play with, no doubt."

"Oh, no," said the Doctor, "thank you. I have a house and garden."

"Yes, Doctor," Dab-Dab put in, "but you wouldn't be bound to buy a second one with the money you would get for the pearls. It would come in real handy for something else, you know."

"The baby spoonbills want them," said John Dolittle. "Why should I take them away from them?"

"Balls of pink putty would suit them just as well," snorted Dab-Dab.

"Putty is poisonous," said the Doctor. "They appreciate the beauty of the pearls. Let them have them. But," he added to the mother spoonbill, "if you know where any more are to be found, I should be glad to know."

"I don't," said she. "I don't even know how these came to be in the possession of the oyster I ate."

"Pearls always grow in oysters—when they grow at all," said the Doctor. "But they are rare. This is the point that most interests me—the natural history of pearls. They are said to form around a grain of sand that gets into the oyster's shell by accident. I had hoped that if you were in the habit of eating oysters you could give me some information."

"I'm afraid I can't," said the spoonbill. "To tell you the truth, I got those oysters from a pile that some other bird had left on the rock here. He had eaten his fill, I suppose, and gone away. There are a good many left still. Let's go over to the pile and crack a few. Maybe they've all got pearls in them."

So they went across to the other side of the little island and started opening oysters. But not another pearl did they find.

"Where are the oyster beds around here?" asked the Doctor.

"Between this island and the next," said the spoonbill. "I don't fish for them myself because I'm not a deep diver. But I've seen other kinds of seabirds fishing in that place— just about halfway between this island and that little one over there."

"I'll go out with her, Doctor," said Dab-Dab, "and do a little fishing on my own account. I can dive pretty deep, though I'm not a regular diving duck. Maybe I can get some pearls for you."

So Dab-Dab went out with the spoonbill and started pearl fishing.

Then for a good hour and a half the faithful housekeeper fished up oyster after oyster and brought them to the Doctor on the island. He and the animals found opening them quite exciting work, because they never knew what they might discover. But nothing was found in the shells but fat oysters and thin oysters.

"I think I'd like to try a hand at diving myself," said the Doctor, "if the water is not too deep. I used to be quite good at fishing up sixpences from the bottom of the swimming pool when I was a boy."

And he took off his clothes, got into the canoe and paddled out with the animals till he was over the oyster beds. Then he dove right down into the clear green water, while Jip and Gub-Gub watched him with intense interest.

But when he came up, blowing like a seal, he hadn't even got an oyster. All he had was a mouthful of seaweed.

"Gub-Gub dives for pearls"

"Let's see what I can do," said Jip. And out of the canoe jumped another pearl fisherman.

Then Gub-Gub got all worked up and before anybody could stop him *he* had taken a plunge. The pig went down so quick and so straight he got his snout stuck in the mud at the bottom, and the Doctor, still out of breath, had to go down after him and get him free. The animals by this time were at such a pitch of excitement that even the white mouse would have jumped in if Gub-Gub's accident hadn't changed his mind.

Jip managed to bring up a few small oysters, but there were no pearls in them.

"I'm afraid we're pretty poor fishers," said John Dolittle. "Of course, it's possible that there may not be any more pearls there."

"No, I'm not satisfied yet," said Dab-Dab. "I'm pretty sure that there are plenty of pearls there—the beds are enormous. I think I'll go around among the seabirds and try to find out who it was got those oysters our spoonbill found the pearls in. The bird that fished up that pile was an expert oyster diver."

So while the Doctor put his clothes on and Gub-Gub washed the mud out of his ears, Dab-Dab went off on a tour of inquiry around the islands.

After about twenty minutes she brought back a black ducklike bird with a tuft on his head.

"This cormorant, Doctor," said she, "fished up that pile of oysters."

"Ah," said John Dolittle, "perhaps we shall find out something now. Can you tell me," he asked the cormorant, "how to get pearls?"

"Pearls? What do you mean?" said the bird.

Then Dab-Dab went and borrowed the playthings from the spoonbill's children to show him.

"Oh, those things," said the cormorant. "Those come in bad oysters. When I go oyster fishing I never pick up that kind except once in a while by accident—and then I never bother to open them."

"But how do you tell oysters of that kind from the others?" asked the Doctor.

"By sniffing them," said the cormorant. "The ones that have those things in them don't smell fresh. I'm frightfully particular about my oysters."

"Do you mean to say that even when you are right down under the water you could tell an oyster that had pearls in it from one that hadn't—just by sniffing it?"

"Certainly. So could any cormorant."

"There you are, Doctor," said Dab-Dab. "The trick's done. Now you can get all the pearls you want."

"But these oyster beds don't belong to me," said John Dolittle.

"Oh, dear!" sighed the duck. "Did anyone ever see a man who could find so many objections to getting rich? Who do they belong to, then?"

"To Chief Nyam-Nyam and his people, of course. He owns the Harmattan Rocks. Would you mind," the Doctor asked, turning to the cormorant, "getting me a few oysters of this kind to look at?"

"With the greatest of pleasure," said the cormorant.

And he flew out over the oyster beds and shot down into the sea like a stone. In a minute he was back again with three oysters—two in his feet and one in his mouth. The animals gathered around with bated breath while the Doctor opened them. In the first was a small gray pearl; in the second a middle-sized pink pearl, and in the third two enormous black ones.

"Gosh, how lovely!" murmured Gub-Gub.

"Pearls before swine," giggled the white mouse. "Tee-hee!"

"How uneducated you are!" snorted the pig, turning up his snout. "Ladies before gentlemen; *swine before pearls!*"

· Chapter 5 ·
OBOMBO'S REBELLION

Late that same afternoon the Doctor returned to Chief Nyam-Nyam's village. And with him he took the cormorant as well as Dab-Dab and his animals.

As he arrived at the little group of straw houses he saw that there was some kind of a commotion going on. All the villagers were gathered about the chief's hut; speeches were being made and everyone seemed in a great state of excitement. The old chief himself was standing at the door, and when he saw his friend, the Doctor, approaching on the edge of the crowd, he signaled him to come into the hut. This the Doctor did. And as soon as he was inside the chief closed the door and began to tell him what the trouble was.

"Great trials have overtaken me in my old age," said he. "For fifty years I have been head of this tribe, respected, honored and obeyed. Now my young son-in-law, Obombo, clamors to be made chief and many of the people support him. Bread we have none; food of any kind is scanty. And Obombo tells the tribesmen that the fault is mine—that he, if he is made chief, will bring them luxury and prosperity. It is not that I am unwilling to give up the chieftaincy, but I know this young upstart who would take my place means to lead the people into war. What can he do by going to war? Can he fill the people's stomachs? In wars we have always lost. Our neighbors are large peoples, while we are the smallest tribe in all West Africa. So we have been robbed and robbed, till now the mothers and children clamor at my door for bread. Alas, alas, that I should ever see this day!"

The old chief sank into his chair as he ended and burst out weeping. The Doctor went up and patted him on the shoulder.

"Chief Nyam-Nyam," said he, "I think I have discovered something today that should make you and your people rich for the remainder of your lives. Go out now and address the tribesmen. Promise them in my name—and remind them that I come recommended by King Koko—promise them from me that if they will abide peacefully under your rule for another week, the country of Chief Nyam-Nyam will be made famous for its riches and prosperity."

Then the old chief opened the door and made a speech to the clamoring crowd outside. And when he had ended Obombo, the son-in-law, got up and began another speech, calling on the people to drive the old man out into the jungle. But before he had got halfway through the crowd began to murmur to one another:

"Let us not listen to this forward young man. It were better far that we abide the Doctor's promise and see what comes. He is a man of deeds, not words. Did he not put the Amazons to flight with a magic mouse that lives in his pocket? Let us side with the Doctor and the venerable Nyam-Nyam, who has ruled us with kindness for so long. Obombo would but lead us into war, and bring us to greater poverty still."

Soon hisses and groans broke out among the crowd and, picking up pebbles and mud, they began pelting Obombo so he could not go on with his speech. Finally he had to run for the jungle himself to escape the fury of the people.

Then when the excitement had died down and the villagers had gone peacefully to their homes, the Doctor told the old chief of the wealth that lay waiting for him in the oysters of the Harmattan Rocks. And the cormorant agreed to oblige John Dolittle by getting a number of his relatives to do pearl fishing for these people, who were so badly in need of money and food.

And during the next week the Doctor paddled the old chief to the rocks twice a day. A great number of oysters were fished up by the cormorants and the pearls were sorted by the Doctor, put in little boxes and sent out to be sold. John Dolittle told the old chief to keep the matter a secret and only to entrust the carrying to reliable men.

And soon money began to pour into the country from the pearl-fishing business, which the Doctor had established, and the people were prosperous and had all the food they wanted.

By the end of that week the Doctor had, indeed, made good his promise. The country of Chief Nyam-Nyam became famous all along the coast of West Africa as a wealthy state.

But wherever money is made in large quantities and business is good, there strangers will always come, seeking their fortune. And before long the little village that used to be so poor and insignificant was full of traders from the neighboring kingdoms, buying and selling in the crowded, busy markets. And, of course, questions were soon asked as to how this country had suddenly gotten so rich. And, although the chief had carried out the Doctor's orders and had only entrusted the secret of the fisheries to a few picked men, folks began to notice that canoes frequently came and went between the Harmattan Rocks and the village of Chief Nyam-Nyam.

Then spies from those neighboring countries who had always been robbing and warring upon this land began to sneak around the rocks in canoes. And, of course, very soon the secret was out.

And the Emir of Ellebubu, who was one of the big, powerful neighbors, called up his army and sent them off in war canoes to take possession of the Harmattan Rocks. At the same time he made an attack upon the village, drove everybody out, and carrying off the Doctor and the chief, he threw them into prison in his own country. Then at last Nyam-Nyam's people had no land left at all.

And in the jungle, where the frightened villagers had fled to hide, Obombo made whispered speeches to little scattered groups of his father-in-law's people, telling them what fools they had been to trust the crazy foreigner, instead of listening to him, who would have led them to greatness.

Now, when the Emir of Ellebubu had thrown the Doctor into prison he had refused to allow Dab-Dab, Jip or Gub-Gub to go with him. Jip put up a fight and bit the emir in the leg. But all he got for that was to be tied up on a short chain.

The prison into which the Doctor was thrown had no

windows. And John Dolittle, although he had been in African prisons before, was very unhappy because he was extremely particular about having fresh air. And besides, his hands were firmly tied behind his back with strong rope.

"Dear me," said he while he was sitting miserably on the floor in the darkness, wondering what on earth he was going to do without any of his animals to help him, "what a poor holiday I am spending, to be sure!"

But presently he heard something stirring in his pocket. And to his great delight, the white mouse, who had been sleeping soundly, entirely forgotten by the Doctor, ran out on his lap.

"Good luck!" cried John Dolittle. "You're the very fellow I want. Would you be so good as to run around behind my back and gnaw this beastly rope? It's hurting my wrists."

"Certainly," said the white mouse, setting to work at once. "Why is it so dark? I haven't slept into the night, have I?"

"No," said the Doctor. "It's only about noon, I should say. But we're locked up. That stupid old Emir of Ellebubu made war on Nyam-Nyam and threw me into jail. Bother it, I always seem to be getting into prison! The worst of it was, he wouldn't let Jip or Dab-Dab come with me. I'm particularly annoyed that I haven't got Dab-Dab. I wish I knew some way I could get a message to her."

"Well, just wait until I have your hands free," said the white mouse. "Then I'll see what can be done. There! I've bitten through one strand. Now wiggle your hands a bit and you can undo the whole rope."

The Doctor squirmed his arms and wrists and presently his hands were free.

"Thank goodness I had you in my pocket!" he said. "That

was a most uncomfortable position. I wonder what kind of a prison old Nyam-Nyam got. This is the worst one I was ever in."

In the meantime the emir, celebrating victory in his palace, gave orders that the Harmattan Rocks, which were now to be called the Royal Ellebubu Pearl Fisheries, would henceforth be his exclusive, private property, and no trespassing would be allowed. And he sent out six special men with orders to take over the islands and to bring all the pearls to him.

Now the cormorants did not know that war had broken out, nor anything about the Doctor's misfortune. And when the emir's men came and took the pearl oysters they had fished up, the birds supposed they were Nyam-Nyam's men and let them have them. However, it happened, luckily, that this first load of oysters had only very small and almost worthless pearls in them.

Jip and Dab-Dab were still plotting to find some way to reach the Doctor. But there seemed to be nothing they could think of.

Inside the prison the Doctor was swinging his arms to get the stiffness out of them.

"You said something about a message you had for Dab-Dab, I think," peeped the white mouse's voice from the darkness of the corner.

"Yes," said the Doctor, "—and a very urgent one. But I don't see how on earth I'm going to get it to her. This place is made of stone and the door's frightfully thick. I noticed it as I came in."

"Don't worry, Doctor, I'll get it to her," said the mouse. "I've just found an old rathole over here in the corner. I popped down it, and it goes under the wall and comes out by the root of the tree on the other side of the road from the prison."

"Oh, how splendid!" cried the Doctor.

"Give me the message," said the white mouse, "and I'll hand it to Dab-Dab before you can say Jack Robinson. She's sitting in the tree, where the hole comes out."

"Tell her," said the Doctor, "to fly over to the Harmattan Rocks right away and give the cormorants strict orders to stop all pearl fishing at once."

"All right," said the mouse. And he slipped down the rathole.

Dab-Dab, as soon as she got the message, went straight off to the pearl fisheries and gave the Doctor's instructions to the cormorants.

She was only just in time. For the emir's six special men were about to land on the islands to get a second load of pearls. Dab-Dab and the cormorants swiftly threw back into the sea the oysters that had been fished up and when the emir's men arrived they found nothing.

After hanging around a while they paddled back and told the emir that they could find no more pearl oysters on the rocks. He sent them out to look again; but they returned with the same report.

Then the emir was puzzled and angry. If Nyam-Nyam could get pearls on the Harmattan Rocks, why couldn't he? And one of his generals said that probably the Doctor had something to do with it, since it was he who had discovered and started the fisheries.

So the emir ordered his hammock men and had himself carried to the Doctor's prison. The door was unlocked and the emir, going inside, said to the Doctor, "What monkey business have you done to my pearl fisheries, you villain?"

"They're not your pearl fisheries, you ruffian," said the Doctor. "You stole them from poor old Nyam-Nyam. The pearls were fished for by diving birds. But the birds are honest and will work only for honest people. Why don't you have windows in your prison? You ought to be ashamed of yourself."

Then the emir flew into a terrible passion.

"How dare you speak to me like that? I am the Emir of Ellebubu," he thundered.

"You're an unscrupulous scoundrel," said the Doctor. "I don't want to talk to you."

"If you don't make the birds work for me I'll give orders that you get no food," said the emir. "You shall be starved to death."

"I have told you," said the Doctor, "that I don't desire any further conversation with you. Not a single pearl shall you ever get from the Harmattan Fisheries."

"And not a bite to eat shall you ever have till I do," the emir yelled.

Then he turned to the prison guards, gave instructions that the Doctor was not to be fed till further orders and stalked out. The door slammed shut with a doleful clang and after one decent breath of fresh air the Doctor was left in the darkness of his stuffy dungeon.

· Chapter 6 ·
THE DOCTOR'S RELEASE

The Emir of Ellebubu went back to his palace feeling perfectly certain that after he had starved John Dolittle for a few days he would be able to make him do anything he wanted. He gave orders that no water should be served to the prisoner either, so as to make doubly sure that he would be reduced to obedience.

But immediately the emir had left, the white mouse started out through the rathole in the corner. And all day and all night he kept busy coming and going, bringing in crumbs of food that he gathered from the houses of the town: bread crumbs, cheese crumbs, yam crumbs, potato crumbs and crumbs of meat that he pulled off bones. All these he stored carefully in the Doctor's hat in the corner of the prison. And by the end of each day he had collected enough crumbs for one good square meal.

The Doctor said he never had the slightest idea of what he was eating, but as the mealy mixture was highly digestible and nutritious he did not see why he should mind. To supply his master with water the mouse got nuts, and after

"The white mouse would roll them down the hole"

gnawing a tiny hole in one end he would chop the nut inside into pieces and shake it out through the hole. Then he would fill the empty shell with water and seal up the hole with gum arabic, which he got from trees. The water-filled nuts were a little heavy for him to carry, so Dab-Dab would bring them from the river as far as the outside end of the rathole, and the white mouse would roll them down the hole into the prison.

By getting his friends, the village mice, to help him in

the preparation of these nuts, he was able to supply them in hundreds. Then all the Doctor had to do when he wanted a drink was to put one in his mouth, crack it with his teeth, and after the cool water had run down his throat, spit the broken shells out.

The white mouse also provided crumbs of soap, so that his master could shave—for the Doctor, even in prison, was always very particular about this part of his appearance.

Well, when four days had passed, the Emir of Ellebubu sent a messenger to the prison to inquire if the Doctor was now willing to do as he was told. The guards after talking to John Dolittle brought word to the emir that the Doctor was as obstinate as ever and had no intention of giving in.

"Very well," said the emir, stamping his foot, "then let him starve. In ten days more the fool will be dead. Then I will come and laugh over him. So perish all wretches who oppose the wishes of the Emir of Ellebubu!"

And in ten days' time he went to the prison, as he had said, to gloat over the terrible fate of his prisoner. Many of his ministers and generals came with him to help him gloat. But when the prison door was opened, instead of seeing the Doctor's body stretched upon the floor, the emir found him smiling on the threshold, shaved and hearty and all spruced up. The only difference in his appearance was that with no exercise in prison he had grown slightly stouter and rounder.

The emir stared at the prisoner open-mouthed, speechless with astonishment. Now, the day before this he had heard for the first time the story of the rout of the Amazons. The emir had refused to believe it. But now he began to feel that anything might be true about this man.

"See," one of the ministers whispered in his ear, "the sorcerer has even shaved his beard without water or soap. Your Majesty, there is surely evil magic here. Set the man free before harm befall. Let us be rid of him."

And the frightened minister moved back among the crowd so the Doctor's evil gaze could not fall upon his face.

Then the emir himself began to get panicky. And he gave orders that the Doctor should be released right away.

"I will not leave here," said John Dolittle, standing squarely in the door, "till you have windows put in this prison. It's a disgrace to lock up anyone in a place without windows."

"Build windows in the prison at once," the emir said to the guards.

"And after that I won't go," said the Doctor. "Not till you have set Chief Nyam-Nyam free; not till you have ordered all your people to leave his country and the Harmattan Rocks; not till you have returned to him the farming lands you robbed him of."

"It shall be done," muttered the emir, grinding his teeth. "Only go!"

"I go," said the Doctor. "But if you ever molest your neighbors again, I will return. Beware!"

Then he strode through the prison door out into the sunlit street, while the frightened people fell back on either side and covered their faces, whispering:

"Magic! Do not let his eye fall on you!"

And in the Doctor's pocket the white mouse had to put his paws over his face to keep from laughing.

And now the Doctor set out with his animals and the old chief to return to Nyam-Nyam's country from the land where he had been imprisoned. On the way they kept meeting with groups of the chief's people who were still hiding in the jungle. These were told the glad tidings of the emir's promise. When they learned that their land was now free and safe again, the people joined the Doctor's party for the return journey. And long before he came in sight of the village John Dolittle looked like a conquering general coming back at the head of an army—so many had gathered to him on the way.

That night grand celebrations were made in the chief's village and the Doctor was hailed by the people as the greatest man who had ever visited their land. Two of their worst enemies need now no longer be feared—the emir had been bound over by a promise and Dahomey was not likely to bother them again after the fright the Amazons got on their last attack. The pearl fisheries were restored to their possession. And the country should now proceed prosperously and happily.

The next day the Doctor went out to the Harmattan Rocks to visit the cormorants and to thank them for the help they had given. The old chief came along on this trip, and with him four trustworthy men of his. In order that there should be no mistake in future, these men were shown to the cormorants and the birds were told to supply them—and no others—with pearl oysters.

While the Doctor and his party were out at the rocks an oyster was fished up that contained an enormous and very beautiful pearl—by far the biggest and handsomest yet found. It was perfect in shape, flawless, and a most unusual shade in color. After making a little speech, the chief presented this pearl to the Doctor as a small return for the services he had done him and his people.

" 'Do you realize what that pearl means to us?' "

"Thank goodness for that!" Dab-Dab whispered to Jip. "Do you realize what that pearl means to us? The Doctor was down to his last shilling—as poor as a church mouse. We would have had to go circus-traveling with the pushmi-pullyu again, if it hadn't been for this. I'm so glad. For, for my part, I shall be glad enough to stay at home and settle down a while—once we get there."

"Oh, I don't know," said Gub-Gub. "I love circuses. I

wouldn't mind traveling, so long as it's in England—and with a circus."

"Well," said Jip, "whatever happens, it's nice the Doctor's got the pearl. He always seems to be in need of money. And, as you say, Dab-Dab, that should make anybody rich for life."

But while the Doctor was still thanking the chief for the beautiful present, Quip-the-Carrier flew up with a letter for him.

"It was marked *Urgent,* in red ink, Doctor," said the swallow, "so Speedy thought he had better send it to you by special delivery."

John Dolittle tore open the envelope.

"Who's it from, Doctor?" asked Dab-Dab.

"Dear me," muttered the Doctor, reading. "It's from that farmer in Lincolnshire whose brussels sprouts we imported for Gub-Gub. I forgot to answer his letter—you remember, he wrote asking me if I could tell him what the trouble was. And I was so busy it went clean out of my mind. Dear me! I must pay the poor fellow back, somehow. I wonder—oh, but there's this. I can send him the pearl. That will pay for his sprouts and something to spare. What a good idea!"

And to Dab-Dab's horror, the Doctor tore a clean piece off the farmer's letter, scribbled a reply, wrapped the pearl up in it, and handed it to the swallow.

"Tell Speedy," said he, "to send that off right away—registered. I am returning to Fantippo tomorrow. Good-bye and thank you for the special delivery."

As Quip-the-Carrier disappeared into the distance with the Doctor's priceless pearl, Dab-Dab turned to Jip and murmured, "There goes the Dolittle fortune. My, but it is marvelous how money *doesn't* stick to that man's fingers!"

"Heigh-ho!" sighed Jip, "it's a circus for us, all right."

"Easy comes, easy goes," murmured Gub-Gub. "Never mind. I don't suppose it's really such fun being rich. Wealthy people have to behave so unnaturally."

· Chapter 7 ·

A MYSTERIOUS LETTER

We are now come to an unusual event in the history of the Doctor's post office, to the one that was, perhaps, the greatest of all the curious things that came about through the institution of the Swallow Mail.

On arriving back at the houseboat from his short and very busy holiday the Doctor was greeted joyfully by the pushmi-pullyu, Too-Too, Cheapside, and Speedy-the-Skimmer. King Koko also came out to greet his friend when he saw the arrival of the Doctor's canoe through a pair of opera glasses which he had recently gotten from London by parcel post. And the prominent Fantippans, who had missed their afternoon tea and social gossip terribly during the postmaster's absence, got into their canoes and followed the King out to the foreign mails office.

So for three hours after his arrival the Doctor did not get a chance to do a thing besides shake hands and answer questions about how he had enjoyed his holiday. The welcome he received on his return and the sight of the comfortable houseboat, gay with flowering window boxes, made the Doctor, as he afterward said to Dab-Dab, feel as though he were really coming home.

"Yes," said the housekeeper, "but don't forget that you have another home, a real one, in Puddleby."

"That's true," said the Doctor. "I suppose I must be getting on to England soon. But the Fantippans were honestly pleased to see us, weren't they? And, after all, Africa is a nice country, now, isn't it?"

"Yes," said Dab-Dab, "a nice enough country for short holidays—and long drinks."

After supper the Doctor had been made to tell the story of the pearl fisheries all over again for the benefit of his own family circle, and he at last turned to the enormous pile of letters that were waiting for him. They came, as usual, from all parts of the world, from every conceivable kind of animal and bird. For hours he waded patiently through them, answering them as they came. Speedy acted as his secretary and took down in bird and animal scribble the answers that the Doctor reeled off by the dozen. Often John Dolittle dictated so fast that the poor Skimmer had to get Too-Too (who had a wonderful memory) to come and help listen, so nothing should be missed through not writing it down quickly enough.

Toward the end of the pile the Doctor came across a very peculiar thick envelope, muddy all over. For a long time none of them could make out a single word of the letter inside, nor even whom it was from. The Doctor got all his notebooks out of the safe, compared and peered and pored over the writing for hours. Mud had been used for ink. The signs were made so clumsily they might almost be anything.

But at last, after a tremendous lot of work—copying out

afresh, guessing, and discussing—the meaning of the extraordinary letter was pieced together, and this is what it said:

Dear Doctor Dolittle:

I have heard of your post office and am writing this as best I can—the first letter I ever wrote. I hear you have a weather bureau in connection with your post office and that a one-eyed albatross is your chief weather prophet. I am writing to tell you that I am the oldest weather prophet in the world. I prophesied the Flood, and it came true to the day and the hour I said it would. I am a very slow walker or I would come and see you and perhaps you could do something for my gout, which in the last few hundred years has bothered me a good deal. But if you will come to see me I will teach you a lot about weather. And I will tell you the story of the Flood, which I saw with my own eyes from the deck of Noah's Ark.

Yours very truly,
Mudface

P.S. I am a turtle.

At last, on reading the muddy message through, the Doctor's excitement and enthusiasm knew no bounds. He began at once to make arrangements to leave the following day for a visit to the turtle.

But, alas, when he turned again to the letter to see where the turtle lived, he could find nothing to give a clue to his whereabouts! The mysterious writer who had seen the Flood, Noah, and the Ark had forgotten to give his address!

"Look here, Speedy," said John Dolittle, "we must try and trace this. Let us leave no stone unturned to find where this valuable document came from. First, we will question everyone in the post office to find out who it was delivered it."

Well, everyone in turn, the pushmi-pullyu, Cheapside, Too-Too, Quip-the-Carrier, all the swallows, any stray birds who were living in the neighborhood, even a pair of rats who had taken up their residence in the houseboat, were cross-examined by the Doctor or Speedy.

But no one had seen the letter arrive; no one could tell what day or hour it had come; no one could guess how it got into the pile of the Doctor's mails; no one knew anything about it. It was one of those little post-office mysteries that are always cropping up even in the best-run mail systems.

The Doctor was positively heartbroken. Often, in his natural history meditations, he had wondered about all sorts of different matters connected with the Ark; and he had decided that Noah, after his memorable voyage was over, must have been a great naturalist. Now a chance to hear the great story from an eyewitness had come most unexpectedly—from someone who had actually known and sailed with Noah—and just because of a silly little slip like leaving out an address the great chance was to be lost!

All attempts to trace the writer having failed, the Doctor, after two days, gave it up and went back to his regular work. This kept him so busy for the next week that he finally forgot all about the turtle and his mysterious letter.

But one night, when he was working late to catch up with the business, which had multiplied during his absence, he heard a gentle tapping on the houseboat window. He left his desk and went and opened it. Instantly in

"In popped the head of an enormous snake"

popped the head of an enormous snake with a letter in its mouth—a thick, muddy letter.

"Great heavens!" cried the Doctor. "What a start you gave me! Come in, come in, and make yourself at home."

Slowly and smoothly the snake slid in over the window-sill and down on to the floor of the houseboat. Yards and yards and more yards long he came, coiling himself up neatly at John Dolittle's feet like a mooring rope on a ship's deck.

"Pardon me, but is there much more of you outside still?" asked the Doctor.

"Yes," said the snake, "only half of me is in yet."

"Then I'll open the door," said the Doctor, "so you can coil part of yourself in the passage. This room is a bit small."

When at last the great serpent was all in, his thick coils entirely covered the floor of the Doctor's office and a good part of him overflowed into the passage outside.

"Now," said the Doctor, closing the window, "what can I do for you?"

"I've brought you this letter," said the snake. "It's from the turtle. He is wondering why he got no answer to his first."

"But he gave me no address," said John Dolittle, taking the muddy envelope from the serpent. "I've been trying my hardest ever since to find out where he lived."

"Oh, was that it?" said the snake. "Well, old Mudface isn't much of a letter writer. I suppose he didn't know he had to give his address."

"I'm awfully glad to hear from him again," said the Doctor. "I had given up all hope of ever seeing him. Can you show me how to get to him?"

"Why, certainly," said the big serpent. "I live in the same lake as he does, Lake Junganyika."

"You're a water snake, then, I take it," said the Doctor.

"Yes."

"You look rather worn-out from your journey. Is there anything I can get you?"

"I'd like a saucer of milk," said the snake.

"I only have wild goats' milk," said John Dolittle. "But it's quite fresh."

And he went out into the kitchen and woke up the house-keeper.

"What do you think, Dab-Dab," he said breathless with excitement, "I've got a second letter from the turtle and the messenger is going to take us to see him!"

When Dab-Dab entered the postmaster's office with the milk she found John Dolittle reading the letter. Looking at the floor, she gave a squawk of disgust.

"It's a good thing for you Sarah isn't here," she cried. "Just look at the state of your office—it's *full of snake*!"

· Chapter 8 ·

THE LAND OF THE MANGROVE SWAMPS

It was a long but a most interesting journey that the Doctor took from Fantippo to Lake Junganyika. It turned out that the turtle's home lay many miles inland in the heart of one of the wildest, most jungly parts of Africa.

The Doctor decided to leave Gub-Gub home this time and he took with him only Jip, Dab-Dab, Too-Too, and Cheapside—who said he wanted a holiday and that his sparrow friends could now quite well carry on the city deliveries in his absence.

The great water snake began by taking the Doctor's party down the coast south for some forty or fifty miles. There they left the sea, entered the mouth of a river and started to journey inland. The canoe (with the snake swimming alongside it) was quite the best thing for this kind of travel so long as the river had water in it. But presently, as they went up it, the stream grew narrower and narrower. Till at last, like many rivers in tropical countries, it was nothing more than the dry bed of a brook, or a chain of small pools with long sandbars between.

Overhead the thick jungle arched and hung like a tunnel of green. This was a good thing by daytime, as it kept the sun off better than a parasol. And in the dry stretches of riverbed, where the Doctor had to carry or drag the canoe on homemade runners, the work was hard and shade something to be grateful for.

The Doctor saw a great deal of new country, trees he had never met before, gay-colored orchids, butterflies, ferns, birds, and rare monkeys. So his notebook was kept busy all the time with sketching and jotting and adding to his already great knowledge of natural history.

On the third day of travel this riverbed led them into a mangrove swamp. It was mournful scenery. Flat bogland, full of pools and streamlets, dotted with tufts of grass and weed, tangled with gnarled roots and brambling bushes, spread out for miles and miles in every direction. No large trees were here, such as they had seen in the jungle lower down. Seven or eight feet above their heads was as high as the mangroves grew and from their thin boughs long streamers of moss hung like gray, fluttering rags.

The life, too, about them was quite different. All manner of swamp birds—big-billed and long-necked, for the most part—peered at them from the sprawling saplings. Many kinds of herons, egrets, ibises, grebes, bitterns—even stately anhingas, who can fly beneath the water—were wading in the swamps or nesting on the little tufty islands. In and out of the holes about the gnarled roots strange and wondrous water creatures—things half fish and half lizard —scuttled and quarreled with brightly colored crabs.

They were glad now that the snake had not allowed them to leave the canoe behind. For here, where every step you took you were liable to sink down in the mud up to your waist, Jip and the Doctor would have had hard work to get along at all without it. And, even with it, the going was slow and hard enough. The mangroves spread out long, twisting, crossing arms in every direction to bar your passage—as though they were determined to guard the secrets of this silent, gloomy land where men could not make a home and seldom ever came.

Indeed, if it had not been for the giant water snake, to whom mangrove swamps were the easiest kind of traveling, they would never have been able to make their way forward. But their guide went on ahead of them for hundreds of yards to lead the way through the best openings and to find the passages where the water was deep enough to float a canoe. And, although his head was out of sight most of the time in the tangled distance, he kept a firm hold on the canoe by taking a turn about the bow post with his tail. And whenever they were stuck in the mud he would contract that long, muscular body of his with a jerk and yank the canoe forward as though it had been no more than a can tied on the end of a string.

Dab-Dab, Too-Too, and Cheapside did not, of course, bother to sit in the canoe. They found flying from tree to tree a much easier way to travel. But in one of these jerky pulls that the snake gave on his living towline, the Doctor and Jip were left sitting in the mud as the canoe was actually yanked from under them. This so much amused the vulgar Cheapside, who was perched in a mangrove tree above their heads, that he suddenly broke the solemn silence of the swamp by bursting into noisy laughter.

"Lor' bless us, Doctor, but you do get yourself into some comical situations! Who would think to see John Dolittle, M.D., heminent physician of Puddleby-on-the-Marsh, bein'

"The canoe was yanked from under them"

pulled through a mud swamp in Africa by a couple of 'undred yards of fat worm! You've no idea how funny you look!"

"Oh, close your silly face!" growled Jip, black mud from head to foot, scrambling back into the canoe. "It's easy for you—you can fly through the mess."

"It 'ud make a nice football ground, this," murmured Cheapside. "I'm surprised the Hafricans 'aven't took to it. I didn't know there was this much mud anywhere—outside of 'Amstead 'Eath after a wet bank 'oliday. I wonder when we're going to get there. Seems to me we're comin' to the end of the world—or the middle of it. 'Aven't seen a 'uman face since we left the shore. 'E's an exclusive kind of gent, our Mr. Turtle, ain't 'e? Meself, I wouldn't be surprised if we ran into old Noah, sitting on the wreck of the Hark, any minute . . . 'Elp the Doctor up, Jip. Look, 'e's got his chin caught under a root."

The snake, hearing Cheapside's chatter, thought something must be wrong. He turned his head-end around and came back to see what the matter was. Then a short halt was made in the journey while the Doctor and Jip cleaned themselves up, and the precious notebooks, which had also been jerked out into the mud, were rescued and stowed in a safe place.

"Do no people at all live in these parts?" the Doctor asked the snake.

"None whatever," said the guide. "We left the lands where men dwell behind us long ago. Nobody can live in these bogs but swamp birds, marsh creatures, and water snakes."

"How much farther have we got to go?" asked the Doctor, rinsing the mud off his hat in a pool.

"About one more day's journey," said the snake. "A wide belt of these swamps surrounds the Secret Lake of Junganyika on all sides. The going will become freer as we approach the open water of the lake."

"We are really on the shores of it already, then?"

"Yes," said the serpent. "But, properly speaking, the Secret Lake cannot be said to have shores at all—or, certainly, as you see, no shore where a man can stand."

"Why do you call it the Secret Lake?" asked the Doctor.

"Because it has never been visited by man since the Flood," said the giant reptile. "You will be the first to see it. We who live in it boast that we bathe daily in the original water of the Flood. For before the Forty Days' Rain came it was not there, they say. But when the Flood passed away this part of the world never dried up. And so it has remained, guarded by these wide mangrove swamps, ever since."

"What was here before the Flood, then?" asked the Doctor.

"They say rolling fertile country, waving corn, and sunny hilltops," the snake replied. "That is what I have heard. I was not there to see. Mudface, the turtle, will tell you all about it."

"How wonderful!" exclaimed the Doctor. "Let us push on. I am most anxious to see him—and the Secret Lake."

· Chapter 9 ·

THE SECRET LAKE

During the course of the next day's travel the country became, as the snake had foretold, freer and more open. Little by little the islands grew fewer and the mangroves not so tangly. In the dreary views there was less land and more water. The going was much easier now. For miles at a stretch the Doctor could paddle, without the help of his guide, in water that seemed to be quite deep. It was indeed a change to be able to look up and see a clear sky overhead once in a while, instead of that everlasting network of swamp trees. Across the heavens the travelers now occasionally saw flights of wild ducks and geese, winging their way eastward.

"That's a sign we're near open water," said Dab-Dab.

"Yes," the snake agreed. "They're going to Junganyika. It is the feeding ground of great flocks of wild geese."

It was about five o'clock in the evening when they came to the end of the little islands and mud banks. And as the canoe's nose glided easily forward into entirely open water they suddenly found themselves looking across a great inland sea.

The Doctor was tremendously impressed by his first sight of the Secret Lake. If the landscape of the swamp country had been mournful this was even more so. No eye could see across it. The edge of it was like the ocean's—just a line where the heavens and the water meet. Ahead to the eastward—the darkest part of the evening sky—even this line barely showed, for now the murky waters and the frowning night blurred together in an inky mass. To the right and left the Doctor could see the fringe of the swamp trees running around the lake, disappearing in the distance north and south.

Out in the open, great banks of gray mist rolled and joined and separated as the wailing wind pushed them fretfully hither and thither over the face of the waters.

"My word!" the Doctor murmured in a quiet voice. "Here one could almost believe that the Flood was not over yet!"

"Jolly place, ain't it?" came Cheapside's cheeky voice from the stern of the canoe. "Give me London any day—in the worst fog ever. This is a bloomin' eels' country. Look at them mist shadows skatin' round the lake. Might be old Noah and 'is family, playin' ring-around-a-rosy in their nightshirts, they're that lifelike."

"The mists are always there," said the snake. "Always have been. In them the first rainbow shone."

"Well," said the sparrow, "I'd sell the whole place cheap if it was mine—mists and all. 'Ow many 'undred miles of this bonny blue ocean 'ave we got to cross before we reach our Mr. Mudface?"

"Not very many," said the snake. "He lives on the edge of

the lake a few miles to the north. Let us hurry and try to reach his home before darkness falls."

Once more, with the guide in front, but this time at a much better pace, the party set off.

As the light grew dimmer the calls of several night birds sounded from the mangroves on the left. Too-Too told the Doctor that many of these were owls, but of kinds that he had never seen or met with before.

"Yes," said the Doctor. "I imagine there are lots of different kinds of birds and beasts in these parts that can be found nowhere else in the world."

At last, while it was still just light enough to see, the snake swung into the left and once more entered the outskirts of the mangrove swamps. Following him with difficulty in the fading light, the Doctor was led into a deep cove. At the end of this the nose of the canoe suddenly bumped into something hard. The Doctor was about to lean out to see what it was when a deep, deep bass voice spoke out of the gloom quite close to him.

"Welcome, John Dolittle. Welcome to Lake Junganyika."

Then looking up, the Doctor saw on a moundlike island the shape of an enormous turtle—fully twelve feet across the shell—standing outlined against the blue-black sky.

The long journey was over at last.

Doctor Dolittle did not at any time believe in traveling with very much baggage. And all that he had brought with him on this journey were a few things rolled up in a blanket—and, of course, the little black medicine bag. Among those things, luckily, however, were a couple of candles. And if it had not been for them, he would have had hard work to land safely from the canoe.

Getting them lighted in the wind that swept across the

"The Doctor saw the shape of an enormous turtle"

lake was no easy matter. But to protect their flame Too-Too wove a couple of little lanterns out of thin leaves, through which the light shone dimly green but bright enough to see your way by.

To his surprise, the Doctor found that the mound, or island, on which the turtle lived was not made of mud, though muddy footprints could be seen all over it. It was made of stone—of stones cut square with a chisel.

While the Doctor was examining them with great

curiosity the turtle said, "They are the ruins of a city. I used to be content to live and sleep in the mud. But since my gout has been so bad I thought I ought to make myself something solid and dry to rest on. Those stones are pieces of a king's house."

"Pieces of a house—of a city!" the Doctor exclaimed, peering into the wet and desolate darkness that surrounded the little island. "But where did they come from?"

"From the bottom of the lake," said the turtle. "Out there," Mudface nodded toward the gloomy wide-stretching waters, "there stood, thousands of years ago, the beautiful city of Shalba. Don't I know, when for long enough I lived in it? Once it was the greatest and fairest city ever raised by men and King Mashtu of Shalba the proudest monarch in the world. Now I, Mudface the turtle, make a nest in the swamp out of the ruins of his palace. Ha-ha!"

"You sound bitter," said the Doctor. "Did King Mashtu do you any harm?"

"I should say he did," growled Mudface. "But that belongs to the story of the Flood. You have come far. You must be weary and in need of food."

"Well," said the Doctor, "I am most anxious to hear the story. Does it take long to tell?"

"About three weeks would be my guess," whispered Cheapside. "Turtles do everything slow. Something tells me that story is the longest story in the world, Doctor. Let's get a nap and a bite to eat first. We can 'ear it just as well tomorrow."

So, in spite of John Dolittle's impatience, the story was put off till the following day. For the evening meal Dab-Dab managed to scout around and gather together quite a nice mess of freshwater shellfish and Too-Too collected some marsh berries that did very well for dessert.

Then came the problem of how to sleep. This was not so easy because, although the foundations of the turtle's mound were of stone, there was hardly a dry spot on the island left where you could lie down. The Doctor tried the canoe. But it was sort of cramped and uncomfortable for sleeping, and now even there, too, the mud had been carried by Dab-Dab's feet and his own. In this country the great problem was getting away from the mud.

"When Noah's family first came out of the Ark," said the turtle, "they slept in little beds that they strung up between the stumps of the drowned trees."

"Ah, hammocks!" cried the Doctor. "Of course—the very thing!"

Then, with Jip's and Dab-Dab's help, he constructed a very comfortable basketwork hammock out of willow wands and fastened it between two larger mangroves. Into this he climbed and drew the blanket over him. Although the trees leaned down toward the water with his weight, they were quite strong and their bendiness acted like good bedsprings.

The moon had now risen and the weird scenery of Junganyika was all green lights and blue shadows. As the Doctor snuffed out his candles and Jip curled himself up at his feet the turtle suddenly started humming a tune in his deep bass voice, waving his long neck from side to side in the moonlight.

"What is that tune you are humming?" asked the Doctor.

"That's the 'Elephants' March,'" said the turtle. "They always played it at the Royal Circus of Shalba for the elephants' procession."

"The trees bent down with his weight"

"Let's 'ope it 'asn't many verses," grumbled Cheapside, sleepily putting his head under his wing.

The sun had not yet risen on the gloomy waters of Lake Junganyika before Jip felt the Doctor stirring in his hammock, preparing to get up.

Presently Dab-Dab could be heard messing about in the mud below, bravely trying to get breakfast ready under difficult conditions.

Next Cheapside, grumbling in a sleepy chirp, brought his

"The Doctor was washing his face in the lake"

head out from under his wing, gave the muddy scenery one look and popped it back again.

But it was of little use to try to get more sleep now. The camp was astir. John Dolittle, bent on the one idea of hearing that story, had already swung himself out of his hammock and was now washing his face noisily in the lake. Cheapside shook his feathers, swore a few words in cockney, and flew off his tree down to the Doctor's side.

"Look 'ere, Doctor," he whispered, "this ain't an 'olesome

place to stay at all. I'm all full of cramp from the damp night air. You'd get webfooted if you loitered in this country long. Listen, you want to be careful about gettin' old Mudface started on his yarn-spinning. D'yer know what 'e reminds me of? Them old Indian-War veterans. Once they begin telling their reminiscences there's no stoppin' 'em. 'E looks like one, too, with that long, scrawny neck of 'is. Tell 'im to make it short and sweet—just to give us the outline of his troubles, like, see? The sooner we can shake the mud of this place off our feet and make tracks for Fantippo the better it'll be for all of us."

Well, when breakfast had been disposed of the Doctor sharpened his pencil, got out a notebook, and—telling Too-Too to listen carefully, in case he should miss anything—he asked the turtle to begin the story of the Flood.

Cheapside had been right. Although it did not take a fortnight to tell, it did take a very full day. Slowly and evenly the sun rose out of the east, passed across the heavens, and sank down into the west. And still Mudface went murmuring on, telling of all the wonders he had seen in days long ago, while the Doctor's pencil wiggled untiringly over the pages of his notebook. The only interruptions were when the turtle paused to lean down and moisten his long throat with the muddy water of the lake, or when the Doctor stopped him to ask a question on the natural history of antediluvian times.

Dab-Dab prepared lunch and supper and served them as silently as she could, so as not to interrupt; but for the Doctor they were very scrappy meals. On into the night the story went. And now John Dolittle wrote by candlelight, while all his pets, with the exception of Too-Too, were already nodding or dozing.

At last, about half past ten—to Cheapside's great relief—the turtle pronounced the final words.

"And that, John Dolittle, is the end of the story of the Flood by one who saw it with his own eyes."

For some time after the turtle finished no one spoke. Even the irreverent Cheapside was silent. Little bits of stars, dimmed by the light of a half-full moon, twinkled like tiny eyes in the dim blue dome that arched across the lake. Away off somewhere among the tangled mangroves an owl hooted from the swamp and Too-Too turned his head quickly to listen. Dab-Dab, the economical house-keeper, seeing the Doctor close his notebook and put away his pencil, blew out the candle.

At last the Doctor spoke: "Mudface, I don't know when, in all my life, I have listened to a story that interested me so much. I—I'm glad I came."

"I too am glad, John Dolittle. You are the only one in the world now who understands the speech of animals. And if you had not come my story of the Flood could not have been told. I'm getting very old and do not ever move far away from Junganyika."

"Would it be too much to ask you?" said the Doctor, "to get me some souvenir from the city below the lake?"

"Not at all," said the turtle. "I'll go down and try to get you something right away."

Slowly and smoothly, like some unbelievable monster of former days, the turtle moved his great bulk across his little island and slid himself into the lake without splash-ing or disturbance of any kind. Only a gentle swirling in the water showed where he had disappeared.

In silence they all waited—the animals now, for the mo-ment, reawakened and full of interest. The Doctor had

"Dab-Dab, the economical housekeeper,
blew out the candle"

visions of his enormous friend moving through the slime
of centuries at the bottom of the lake, hunting for some
souvenir of the great civilization that passed away with the
Flood. He hoped that he would bring a book or something
with writing on it.

Instead, when at last he reappeared wet and shining in
the moonlight, he had a carved stone windowsill on his
back that must have weighed over a ton.

"Lor' bless us!" muttered Cheapside. "What a wonderful piano mover 'e would make, to be sure! Great Carter Patterson! Does 'e think the Doctor's goin' to 'ang that on 'is watch chain?"

"It was the lightest thing I could find," said the turtle, rolling it off his back with a thud that shook the island. "I had hoped I could get a vase or a plate or something you could carry. But all the smaller objects are now covered in fathoms of mud. This I broke off from the second story of the palace—from the queen's bedroom window. I thought perhaps you'd like to see it anyway, even if it was too much for you to carry home. It's beautifully carved. Wait till I wash some of the mud off it."

The candles were lighted again and after the carvings had been cleaned the Doctor examined them with great care and even made sketches of some of them in his notebook.

By the time the Doctor had finished, all his party, excepting Too-Too, had fallen asleep. It was only when he heard Jip suddenly snore from the hammock that he realized how late it was. As he blew out the candles again he found that it was very dark, for now the moon had set. He climbed into bed and drew the blankets over him.

· Chapter 10 ·

THE POSTMASTER-GENERAL'S
LAST ORDER

When Dab-Dab roused the party the next morning the sun was shining through the mist upon the lake, doing its best to brighten up the desolate scenery around them.

Poor Mudface awoke with an acute attack of gout. He had not been bothered by this ailment since the Doctor's arrival. But now he could scarcely move at all without great pain. And Dab-Dab brought his breakfast to him where he lay.

John Dolittle was inclined to blame himself for having asked him to go hunting in the lake for souvenirs the night before.

"I'm afraid that was what brought on the attack," said the Doctor, getting out his little black bag from the canoe and mixing some medicines. "But you know you really ought to move out of this damp country to some drier climate. I am aware that turtles can stand an awful lot of wet. But at your age one must be careful, you know."

"There isn't any other place I like as well," said Mudface.

HUGH LOFTING

"Mixing the turtle's medicine"

"It's so hard to find a country where you're not disturbed these days."

"Here, drink this," the Doctor ordered, handing him a teacup full of some brown mixture. "I think you will find that that will soon relieve the stiffness in your front legs."

The turtle drank it down. And in a minute or two he said he felt much better and could now move his legs freely without pain.

"It's a wonderful medicine, that," said he. "You are surely a great Doctor. Have you got any more of it?"

"I will make up several bottles of the mixture and leave them with you before I go," said John Dolittle. "But you really ought to get on high ground somewhere. This muddy little hummock is no place for you to live. Isn't there a regular island in the lake, where you could make your home—if you're determined not to leave the Jungan-yika country?"

"Not one," said the turtle. "It's all like this, just miles and miles of mud and water. I used to like it—in fact I do still. I wouldn't wish for anything better if it weren't for this wretched gout of mine."

"Well," said the Doctor, "if you haven't got an island we must make one for you."

"Make one!" cried the turtle. "How would you go about it?"

"I'll show you very shortly," said John Dolittle. And he called Cheapside to him.

"Will you please fly down to Fantippo," he said to the city manager, "and give this message to Speedy-the-Skim-mer. And ask him to send it out to all the postmasters of the branch offices: The Swallow Mail is very shortly to be closed—at all events for a considerable time. I must now be returning to Puddleby and it will be impossible for me to continue the service in its present form after I have left No-Man's-Land. I wish to convey my thanks to all the birds, postmasters, clerks, and letter carriers who have so generously helped me in this work. The last favor that I am going to ask of them is a large one; and I hope they will give me their united support in it. I want them to build me an island in the middle of Lake Junganyika. It is for

Mudface the turtle, the oldest animal living, who in days gone by did a very great deal for man and beast—for the whole world, in fact—when the earth was passing through the darkest chapters in all its history. Tell Speedy to send word to all bird leaders throughout the world. Tell him I want as many birds as possible right away to build a healthy home where this brave turtle may end his long life in peace. It is the last thing I ask of the post-office staff, and I hope they will do their best for me."

Cheapside said that the message was so long he was afraid he would never be able to remember it by heart. So John Dolittle told him to take it down in bird scribble and he dictated it to him all over again.

That letter, the last circular order issued by the great postmaster general to the staff of the Swallow Mail, was treasured by Cheapside for many years. He hid it under his untidy nest in St. Edmund's left ear on the south side of the chancel of St. Paul's Cathedral. He always hoped that the pigeons who lived in the front porch of the British Museum would someday get it into the museum for him. But one gusty morning, when men were cleaning the outside of the cathedral, it got blown out of St. Edmund's ear and, before Cheapside could overtake it, it sailed over the housetops into the river and sank.

The sparrow got back to Junganyika late that afternoon. He reported that Speedy, on receiving the Doctor's message, had immediately forwarded it to the postmasters of the branch offices with orders to pass it on to all the bird leaders everywhere. It was expected that the first birds would begin to arrive here early the following morning.

It was Speedy himself who woke the Doctor at dawn the next day. And while breakfast was being eaten he explained to John Dolittle the arrangements that had been made.

The work, the Skimmer calculated, would take three days. All birds had been ordered to pick up a stone or a pebble or a pinch of sand from the seashore on their way and bring it with them. The larger birds (who would carry stones) were to come first, then the middle-sized birds, and then the little ones with sand.

Soon, when the sky over the lake was beginning to fill up with circling ospreys, herons, and albatrosses, Speedy left the Doctor and flew off to join them. There, taking up a position in the sky right over the center of the lake, he hovered motionless, as a marker for the stone droppers. Then the work began.

All day long a never-ending stream of big birds, a dozen abreast, flew up from the sea and headed across Lake Junganyika. The line was like a solid black ribbon, the birds, dense, packed, and close, beak to tail. And as each dozen reached the spot where Speedy hovered, twelve stones dropped into the water. The procession was so continuous and unbroken that it looked as though the sky were raining stones. And the constant roar of them splashing into the water out of the heavens could be heard a mile off.

The lake in the center was quite deep. And of course tons and tons of stone would have to be dropped before the new island would begin to show above the water's surface. This gathering of birds was greater even than the one the Doctor had addressed in the hollow of No-Man's-Land. It was the biggest gathering of birds that had ever been seen. For now not only the leaders came but thousands and millions of every species. John Dolittle got tremendously excited and, jumping into his canoe, he started to paddle out

"A never-ending stream of big birds"

nearer to the work. But Speedy grew impatient that the top of the stone pile was not yet showing above the water; and he gave the order to double up the line—and then double again, as still more birds came to help from different parts of the world. And soon, with a thousand stones falling every fraction of a second, the lake got so rough that the Doctor had to put back for the turtle's hummock lest his canoe capsize.

All that day, all that night and half the next day, this

continued. At last about noon on the morrow the sound of the falling stones began to change. The great mound of seething white water, like a fountain in the middle of the lake, disappeared; and in its place a black spot showed. The noise of splashing changed to the noise of stone rattling on stone. The top of the island had begun to show.

"It's like the mountains peeping out after the Flood," Mudface muttered to the Doctor.

Then Speedy gave the order for the middle-sized birds to join in; and soon the note of the noise changed again—shriller—as tons and tons of pebbles and gravel began to join the downpour.

Another night and another day went by, and at dawn the gallant Skimmer came down to rest his weary wings; for the workers did not need a marker any longer—now that a good-sized island stood out on the bosom of the lake for the birds to drop their burdens on.

Bigger and bigger grew the homemade land, and soon Mudface's new estate was acres wide. Still another order from Speedy, and presently the rattling noise changed to a gentle hiss. The sky now was simply black with birds. The pebble shower had ceased; it was raining sand. Last of all, the birds brought seeds: grass seeds, the seeds of flowers, acorns, and the kernels of palms. The turtle's new home was to be provided with turf, with wild gardens, with shady avenues to keep off the African sun.

When Speedy came to the hummock and said, "Doctor, it is finished," Mudface gazed thoughtfully out into the lake and murmured:

"Now proud Shalba is buried indeed: she has an island for a tombstone! It's a grand home you have given me, John Dolittle. Alas, poor Shalba!—Mashtu the king passes. But Mudface the turtle . . . lives on!"

· Chapter 11 ·

GOOD-BYE TO FANTIPPO

Mudface's landing on his new home was quite an occasion. The Doctor paddled out alongside of him till they reached the island. Until he set foot on it, John Dolittle himself had not realized what a large piece of ground it was. It was more than a quarter of a mile across. Round in shape, it rose gently from the shores to the flat center, which was a good hundred feet above the level of the lake.

Mudface was tremendously pleased with it. Climbing laboriously to the central plateau—from where you could see great distances over the flat country around—he said he was sure his health would quickly improve in this drier air.

Dab-Dab prepared a meal—the best she could in the circumstances—to celebrate what she called the turtle's housewarming. And everyone sat down to it; and there was much gaiety and the Doctor was asked to make a speech in honor of the occasion.

Cheapside was dreadfully afraid that Mudface would get

"Dab-Dab prepared a meal"

up to make a speech in reply and that it would last into the following day. But to the sparrow's relief the Doctor, as soon as he had finished, prepared for his departure.

He made up the six bottles of gout mixture and presented them to Mudface with instructions in how it should be taken. He told him that although he was closing up the post office for regular service it would always be possible to get word to Puddleby. He would ask several birds of passage to stop here occasionally; and if the gout got any worse he wanted Mudface to let him know by letter.

The old turtle thanked him over and over again and the parting was a very affecting one. When at last the good-byes were all said, they got into the canoe and set out on the return journey.

Reaching the mouth of the river at the southern end of the lake they paused a moment before entering the man-grove swamps and looked back. And there in the distance they could just see the shape of the old turtle standing on his new island, watching them. They waved to him and pushed on.

"He looks just the same as we saw him the night we arrived," said Dab-Dab. "You remember? Like a statue on a pedestal against the sky."

"Poor old fellow!" murmured the Doctor. "I do hope he will be all right now. . . . What a wonderful life! What a wonderful history!"

"Didn't I tell you, Doctor," said Cheapside, "that it was going to be the longest story in the world? Took a day and 'alf a night to tell."

"Ah, but it's a story that nobody else could tell," said John Dolittle.

"Good thing too," muttered the sparrow. "It would never do if there was many of 'is kind spread around this busy world. Of course, meself, I don't believe a word of the yarn. I think 'e made it all up. 'E 'ad nothin' else to do—sittin' there in the mud, century after century, cogitatin'."

The journey down through the jungle was completed without anything special happening. But when they reached the sea and turned the bow of the canoe westward they came upon a very remarkable thing. It was an enormous hole in the beach—or rather a place where the beach had been taken away bodily. Speedy told the Doctor that it was here that the birds had picked up the stones and sand on their way to Junganyika. They had literally carried acres of the seashore nearly a thousand miles inland. Of course in a few months the action of the surf filled in the hole, so that the place looked like the rest of the beach.

But that is why, when many years later some learned geologists visited Lake Junganyika, they said that the seashore gravel on an island there was a clear proof that the sea had once flowed through that neighborhood. Which was true—in the days of the Flood. But the Doctor was the only scientist who knew that Mudface's island, and the stones that made it, had quite a different history.

On his arrival at the post office the Doctor was given his usual warm reception by the king and dignitaries of Fantippo, who paddled out from the town to welcome him back.

Tea was served at once; and His Majesty seemed so delighted at renewing this pleasant custom that John Dolittle was loath to break the news to him that he must shortly resign from the foreign mail service and sail for England. However, while they were chatting on the veranda of the houseboat a fleet of quite large sailing vessels entered the harbor. These were some of the new merchant craft of Fantippo that plied regularly up and down the coast, trading with other African countries. The Doctor pointed out to the King that mails intended for foreign lands could now be quite easily taken by these boats to the bigger ports on the coast, where vessels from Europe called every week.

From that the Doctor went on to explain to the King,

that much as he loved Fantippo and its people, he had many things to attend to in England and must now be thinking of going home. And of course as none of the natives could talk bird language, the Swallow Mail would have to be replaced by the ordinary kind of post office.

The Doctor found that His Majesty was much more distressed at the prospect of losing his good friend and his afternoon tea on the houseboat than at anything else which the change would bring. But he saw that the Doctor really felt he had to go; and at length, with tears falling into his teacup, he gave permission for the postmaster general of Fantippo to resign.

Great was the rejoicing among the Doctor's pets and the patient swallows when the news got about that John Dolittle was really going home at last. Gub-Gub and Jip could hardly wait while the last duties and ceremonies of closing the houseboat to the public and transferring the foreign mails service to the office in the town were performed. Dab-Dab bustled cheerfully from morning to night, while Cheapside never ceased to chatter of the glories of London, the comforts of a city life, and all the things he was going to do as soon as he got back to his beloved native haunts.

There was no end to the complimentary ceremonies that the good King Koko and his courtiers performed to honor the departing Doctor. For days and days, canoes came and went between the town and the houseboat bearing presents to show the goodwill of the Fantippans. Having to keep smiling the whole time, the Doctor got sadder and sadder at leaving his good friends. And he was heartily glad when the hour came to pull up the anchor and put to sea.

People who have written the history of the Kingdom of

HUGH LOFTING

"A wooden statue still stands in his memory"

Fantippo all devote several chapters to a mysterious man who made enormous improvements in the mail, the communications, the shipping, the commerce, the education, and the general prosperity of the country. Indeed, it was through John Dolittle's quiet influence that King Koko's reign came to be looked upon as the Golden Age in Fantippan history. A wooden statue still stands in the marketplace in his memory.

• • •

The excellent postal service continued after he left. The stamps with Koko's face on them were as various and as beautiful as ever. On the occasion of the first annual review of the Fantippo merchant fleet a very fine two-shilling stamp was struck in commemoration, showing His Majesty inspecting his new ships through a lollipop quizzing glass. The King himself became a stamp collector and his album was as good as a family photo album, containing as it did so many pictures of himself. The only awkward incident that happened in the record of the post office that the Doctor had done so much to improve was when some ardent stamp collectors, wishing to make the modern stamps rare, plotted to have the King assassinated in order that the current issues should go out of date. But the plot was, happily, discovered before any harm was done.

Years afterward, the birds visiting Puddleby told the Doctor that the King still had the flowers in the window boxes of his old houseboat carefully tended and watered in his memory. His Majesty, they said, never gave up the fond hope that someday his good friend would come back to Fantippo with his kindly smile, his instructive conversation, and his jolly tea parties on the post-office veranda.

THE END

· Afterword ·

It has been some time since the Doctor Dolittle books have been published in this country. While they continued to sell millions of copies in more than a dozen languages around the world, ironically in the United States, where this world-renowned story of the doctor who learned to speak the animal languages was first published, the books have been out of print for more than a decade.

It was, therefore, particularly gratifying when Dell announced plans to bring back the Doctor Dolittle books. Once more Doctor Dolittle, Tommy Stubbins, Matthew Mugg, and the Doctor's animal family from Puddleby-on-the-Marsh—Polynesia the parrot, Dab-Dab the duck, Jip the dog, Too-Too the owl, Chee-Chee the monkey—will be sharing their adventures with a whole new generation of young readers.

When it was decided to reissue the Doctor Dolittle books, we were faced with a challenging opportunity and decision. In some of the books there were certain incidents depicted that, in light of today's sensitivities, were considered by some to be disrespectful to ethnic minorities and, therefore, perhaps inappropriate for today's young reader. In these centenary editions, this issue is addressed.

The problem that the editors at Dell faced was whether or not to delete or rewrite portions of the Doctor Dolittle stories. Publishers rightfully believe that it is their job to publish a writer's work, not to act as censors. Because the author is no longer living, it was impossible to obtain his permission to make changes. The Doctor Dolittle stories are, moreover, classics of children's literature, and on principle one can make a strong argument that one should not tamper with the classics.

Yet times have changed. Is it appropriate to reissue the Doctor Dolittle books exactly as written and stand on principle at the expense of our obligation to respect the feelings of others? Should future generations of children be denied the opportunity to read the Doctor Dolittle stories because of a few minor references in one or two of the books which were never intended by the author to comment on any ethnic group, particularly when the references are not an integral or important part of the story? What should our response be when there is widespread disagreement among well-meaning parents, librarians, and teachers as to the proper action to take?

Book banning or censorship is not an American tradition! To change the original could be interpreted as censorship. Then again, so could a decision to deny children access to an entire series of classics on the basis of isolated passing references. These were the difficulties we faced when trying to decide whether or not to reissue the Doctor Dolittle books and, if we did, whether or not it was appropriate to make changes in the original version.

After much soul-searching the consensus was that

changes should be made. The deciding factor was the strong belief that the author himself would have immediately approved of making the alterations. Hugh Lofting would have been appalled at the suggestion that any part of his work could give offense and would have been the first to have made the changes himself. In any case, the alterations are minor enough not to interfere with the style and spirit of the original.

In addition, some of the original illustrations from the book have been deleted and others—also original Hugh Lofting illustrations never before published in book form —have been added.

The message that Hugh Lofting conveyed throughout his work was one of respect for life and the rights of all who share the common destiny of our world. That theme permeates the entire Doctor Dolittle series. I would like to acknowledge the following editors whose faith in the literary value of these children's classics was invaluable in the publication of the new editions: Janet Chenery, consulting editor; Olga Fricker, Hugh Lofting's sister-in-law, who worked closely with the author and edited the last four original books; Lori Mack, associate editor at Dell; and Lois Myller, whose special love for Doctor Dolittle helped make this project possible. If our alterations help to refocus Hugh Lofting's intended lessons to his young audience, we will know our decision was the right one.

Christopher Lofting

· About the Author ·

HUGH LOFTING was born in Maidenhead, England, in 1886 and was educated at home with his brothers and sister until he was eight. He studied engineering in London and at the Massachusetts Institute of Technology. After his marriage in 1912 he settled in the United States.

During World War One he left his job as a civil engineer, was commissioned a lieutenant in the Irish Guards, and found that writing illustrated letters to his children eased the strain of war. "There seemed to be very little to write to youngsters from the front; the news was either too horrible or too dull. One thing that kept forcing itself more and more upon my attention was the very considerable part the animals were playing in the war. That was the beginning of an idea: an eccentric country physician with a bent for natural history and a great love of pets. . . ."

These letters became *The Story of Doctor Dolittle*, published in 1920. Children all over the world have read this book and the eleven that followed, for they have been translated into almost every language. *The Voyages of Doctor Dolittle* won the Newbery Medal in 1923. Drawing from the twelve Doctor Dolittle volumes, Hugh Lofting's sister-in-law, Olga Fricker, later compiled *Doctor Dolittle: A Treasury*, which was published by Dell in 1986 as a Yearling Classic.

Hugh Lofting died in 1947 at his home in Topanga, California.